The Last Judgment of Kings / Le Jugement dernier des rois

*Scènes francophones: Studies in French
and Francophone Theater*

Series editor: Logan J. Connors, University of Miami

Dedicated to scholarship on French-language theater, *Scènes francophones* publishes theoretically and historically informed research on dramatic texts and productions from medieval France to the contemporary French-speaking world. Linguistically focused but broad in scope, this series features monographs and multiauthored volumes on dramatic literatures, theories, and practices.

Scènes francophones, which publishes in English, welcomes new research on specific playwrights or actors as well as analysis of particular theaters, dramatic repertoires, and performance spaces. Research in which theater plays a leading role among other genres, themes, or institutions is also encouraged. This series supports research on the social, economic, and cultural history of theater across time periods, from hexagonal France to the reaches of the French-speaking world today.

Recent titles in the series:

The Last Judgment of Kings / Le Jugement dernier des rois: A Bilingual Edition
Sylvain Maréchal
Yann Robert, ed. and trans.

Contemporary Francophone African Plays: An Anthology
Judith G. Miller with Sylvie Chalaye, eds.

Modes of Play in Eighteenth-Century France
Fayçal Falaky and Reginald McGinnis, eds.

Mormons in Paris: Polygamy on the French Stage, 1874–1892
Corry Cropper and Christopher M. Flood, eds.

Playing the Martyr: Theater and Theology in Early Modern France
Christopher Semk

Acting Up: Staging the Subject in Enlightenment France
Jeffrey M. Leichman

For more information about the series, please visit bucknelluniversitypress.org.

Additional Praise for *The Last Judgment of Kings /
Le Jugement dernier des rois: A Bilingual Edition*

"Making this hard-to-find text accessible to both Francophone
and Anglophone readers, this fantastically helpful new edition
and translation also includes a substantial critical introduction,
which demonstrates how this play—frequently cited, but all-
too-rarely engaged with in detail—is at once much more complex, and much more fertile than previous scholars have tended
to allow. A collaborative project with three generations of students, this is also a wonderful pedagogical model that reveals
the value of bringing research material into the classroom."
—Jessica Goodman, editor and
translator of *The Philosophes*

"A superb edition and lively translation of one of the French
Revolution's most striking plays. In his expert introduction,
Yann Robert carefully lays out the theatrical and political
contexts, bringing this subversive comedy to life for readers of
all levels." —Thomas Wynn, author of *Reading Drama in
Eighteenth-Century France*

"This innovative and erudite edition restores Sylvain Maréchal's
astonishing and wildly comic play to a rightful place of promi-
nence while breaking new ground with a new, student-led collective translation. Yann Robert's book is a brilliant example of
how scholarship can align with the teaching of the French
Revolution's endlessly fascinating theater."
—Annelle Curulla, author of *Gender and
Religious Life in French Revolutionary Drama*

"Sylvain Maréchal's *Le Jugement dernier des rois* was the most
important play performed during the French Revolution, yet it
is surprisingly little-known. Scholars and students alike will
therefore warmly welcome this new edition and translation of

the play, for which editor Yann Robert has supplied a sparkling introduction." —Colin Jones, author of *The Fall of Robespierre: 24 Hours in Revolutionary Paris*

"Robert offers a wonderfully engaging and readable English translation of one of the most original and incendiary plays of the French Revolution.

"While the script provides a front-row seat to how theater shaped and was shaped by the new social and political order of the French Revolution, the volume's introduction and critical apparatus provide essential contextualizing information on the main debates both of the Revolutionary period and of revolutionary scholarship today. Robert argues convincingly for the play's unique presentation of the issues of the day, and at times corrects the scholarly record on it.

"In short, the volume offers an illuminating window onto theatre's role and inventiveness at a highly charged and precarious moment of the Revolution, as well as an innovative and portable pedagogical model for collaborative translation. With so few plays of the Revolution available in English translation, this is a welcome and valuable addition for teachers, scholars, and students alike." —Cecilia Feilla, author of *The Sentimental Theater of the French Revolution*

SYLVAIN MARÉCHAL

The Last Judgment of Kings / Le Jugement dernier des rois

A Bilingual Edition

EDITED AND TRANSLATED BY YANN ROBERT

BUCKNELL
UNIVERSITY PRESS
LEWISBURG, PENNSYLVANIA

978-1-68448-544-4 (paper)
978-1-68448-545-1 (cloth)
978-1-68448-546-8 (ePUB)
978-1-68448-547-5 (Web PDF)

Cataloging-in-publication data is available from the Library of Congress.
LCCN 2024947093

A British Cataloging-in-Publication record for this book is available
from the British Library.

References to internet websites (URLs) were accurate at the time of writing.
Neither the author nor Bucknell University Press is responsible for URLs that may
have expired or changed since the manuscript was prepared.

♾ The paper used in this publication meets the requirements of the American
National Standard for Information Sciences—Permanence of Paper for Printed
Library Materials, ANSI Z39.48-1992.

bucknelluniversitypress.org

Distributed worldwide by Rutgers University Press

To my students, whose dedication made this book, and its dedication, possible.

CONTENTS

A COLLABORATIVE TRANSLATION

This translation is unusual in that it was completed as a collaboration involving twenty-seven undergraduate and graduate students over the course of five years and three separate classes at the University of Illinois Chicago. It began in the spring of 2018, when I sought to provide the students in a seminar entitled "The Conflicted Enlightenment" with a greater variety of assignments by requesting that they not only read and analyze Maréchal's *Jugement dernier des rois* but that each also translate a few pages from it. The act of translating short sections engaged the students (whose names are listed below) in a different relationship to the text, encouraging them to focus less on plot and more on style and diction. Even just a few pages of translation improved their analysis of the play as a whole, as they became more attuned to fluctuations in language between sections and between characters. It drew their attention, for instance, to one of the most singular characteristics of the play, which I would describe as "Robespierre meets Hébert": long passages of the florid, verbose prose typical of Revolutionary orators interspersed with much more succinct, colloquial speech, at times bordering on slang ("Tenez, faquins, voilà de la pâture. Bouffez"). This stylistic variety only rendered more salient the greatest dilemma faced by translators of old texts—whether and how much to modernize the style. The students and I debated this thorny issue before starting to translate and decided to preserve whenever possible the distinctive grandiloquence of Revolutionary oration but to err when in doubt on the side of fluency and clarity. We wanted Anglophone readers to have a similar experience to French speakers reading the original play—the sense of encountering something unfamiliar, born of a unique cultural moment—but without it sounding *too* unfamiliar, too foreign and stilted, as it would have if we had slavishly reproduced the distinctly French sentence structure and length of the sans-culottes' political declamations.

To give one example that elicited much debate: the sentence "Eh! Dans quelle trame odieuse, dans quelle intrigue criminelle les prêtres et leur chef n'ont-ils pas pris part, n'ont-ils pas joué un rôle?" beautifully illustrates the common practice in Revolutionary oration of repeating synonyms in quick succession for emphasis ("trame odieuse" and "intrigue criminelle"; "pris part" and "joué un rôle"). A student's first attempt at a translation— "Eh! In what despicable plot, in what criminal scheme did the priests and their leader not take part, did they not play a role?"— struck me as overly literal, even after deleting the wholly superfluous "did they." The repetition of "not take part . . . not play a role," in particular, had an unnatural ring to it in English. I proposed splitting the sentence into two: "Eh! In what despicable plot did the priests and their leader not take part? In what criminal scheme did they not play a role?" Some students expressed concern that this represented too significant a departure from the French text. Others liked that it preserved the lofty vocabulary and repetitiveness of the original passage while avoiding its confusing (in English) syntax. In the absence of a perfect solution and after considerable discussion, we opted for the clarity and fluency of two sentences over the greater accuracy of a single, but stilted, sentence.

A few years later, in the fall of 2021, after reading and correcting once more the first draft of our translation, I settled on a different approach for my next graduate seminar, "Political Theater: From the Sun King to the Terror." While this new group of students also contributed to the translation—as the first to read the English version of the play in one sitting rather than in short fragments, they proved particularly adept at finding the typographical and stylistic inconsistencies that inevitably arise with so many translators—the focus of our work shifted from the translation proper to the reasons why this dramatic work deserved to be translated. I shared with the students my conviction that this play more than any others, due to its brevity, generic hybridity, thematic complexity, and contentious performance history, could provide an ideal entryway into the most noteworthy debates of the French Revolution. I identified the open-ended questions raised by *The Last Judgment of Kings*, invited each student to choose their favorite, and asked them to find at least one primary source (newspaper report, pamphlet, governmental document, etc.) and one secondary source related to the topic they had selected. Each week one student presented their findings to the class, enabling us to study, through Maréchal's play (and through other readings for that week), a new facet of Revolutionary thought and history. So productive was this approach that I decided to organize my introduction to the edition around the same broad questions, designed to highlight ongoing debates in the field of Revolutionary studies rather than offer an individual, restrictive interpretation of the play. For my students, *The Last Judgment of Kings* and our efforts at contextualizing it opened a series of portals through which to explore Revolutionary conceptions of justice, time, religion, commemoration, laughter, and propaganda—a journey into the past that we hope other classes will undertake through this edition, with its introduction as a travel guide.

If the first set of students served as translators and the second as researchers, then the third and final group performed the duties of editors. In the fall of 2022, I taught a graduate seminar on French grammar and composition, a class that partly relies on translation to attune the ears of non-native French speakers to subtle differences in style, register, and diction. Here was a chance, then, to take an exercise largely disconnected from the world beyond the classroom (especially when translating disjointed sentences from a grammar textbook) and turn it instead into a more meaningful activity, in which the students knew that their decisions would have a genuine impact on a publication with a more substantial lifespan and readership than just a single semester and professor. I redesigned the syllabus so that each week the students would read a few pages of the original play and its translation at home, comparing the two texts line by line and marking words or phrases in need of improvement. Among other strategies, I taught them to consult eighteenth-century dictionaries and encyclopedias to determine the meaning of archaic terms ("modérantiser") and of words whose definitions had changed over the centuries, such as "s'embrasser" (now mainly "to kiss," previously "to hug"), "embêter" (now "to annoy," previously "to make stupid or blind"), and "sans doute" (now "probably," previously "certainly"). During class, the students shared the passages that had seemed unnatural or inaccurate to them and debated whether a change was in fact required and for what reason (semantics, rhythm, register, etc.) before proposing and voting on alternate translations. Four years had passed since the initial translation, a span of time that proved helpful in two regards: first, by making it possible for a significant number of students with diverse strengths and opinions to collaborate, and second, by anonymizing the editorial work of the later classes. Indeed, the students in the third seminar had never met any of the original translators, making it easier for them to critique and change (sometimes drastically) passages that were not associated in their minds with a known peer. Editing a friend's prose is notoriously tricky, and editing one's own even more so; splitting the task of translating and revising between different groups thus facilitated more productive discussions and a smoother collaboration.

Among the many students who made this edition possible, two deserve special thanks and recognition. In the summer of 2018, Diane Rae McQueen volunteered to compile and then read the twelve fragments of translation, offering invaluable suggestions at a time when the different sections still lacked any typographical or stylistic cohesion. In fall 2022 and spring 2023, I hired Julianne Angeli as a research associate, a title that fails to capture the many vital roles that she played in the completion of this project, such as tracking down and digitizing hard-to-find primary and secondary sources, revising and harmonizing the translation one more time, and researching many of the play's French and English footnotes. I could not have hoped for more astute and conscientious collaborators, and my experience working with them and with the students listed below have shown me that there is much to be gained in jettisoning the "lone scholar" model that still dominates research in the humanities in favor of a more cooperative approach.[1]

Students in "The Conflicted Enlightenment" (spring 2018)— the original translators

Julianne Brooks

Rebecca Ebling

Adam Erickson

Sara Ghazi Filali

Diane Rae McQueen

Samar Miled

Carmen Morales

Kevin Nonin

Kevin Orr

Dayana Salazar

Sarah Schaefer

Yasmine Toledo

Students in "Political Theater: From the Sun King to the Terror" (fall 2021)—the researchers

Julianne Angeli

Stephanie Beauval

Angela Chidlow

Ciat Conlin

Aisha Craig

Crystal Figueroa

Elena Guritanu

Marie Soupart

Students in "French in Style: Advanced Speaking, Writing and Research" (fall 2022)—the editors

Stephanie Diaz

Kolade Kenneth

Zack Martin

Cynthia Okoye

Grace Pnacek

Jackie Wilson

Julian Wrobel

NOTE

1. Jessica Goodman likewise advocates a more cooperative approach and illustrates its value beautifully in her own collaborative translation of an eighteenth-century French play with six undergraduate students. Charles Palissot, *The Philosophes*, ed. Jessica Goodman and Olivier Ferret, trans. Jessica Goodman et al. (Cambridge, UK: Open Book Publishers, 2021).

*The Last Judgment of
Kings / Le Jugement
dernier des rois*

INTRODUCTION

Ever since its premiere in October 1793, Sylvain Maréchal's *The Last Judgment of Kings* has been held up (and put down) by historians and literary critics alike as the epitome of Revolutionary drama.[1] While the absence of a stand-alone affordable edition[2] has meant it remains rarely read and almost never performed, Maréchal's short, carnivalesque play continues to be the most frequently cited theatrical work of the French Revolution.[3] Certain elements of its plot, such as the burlesque procession of real-life European leaders, from Catherine the Great and George III to Pope Pius VI, their farcical brawl over a barrel of crackers, and above all the memorable ending that sees them all engulfed by the eruption of a volcano onstage, are familiar to all specialists of the Revolution and its theater. Anecdotal accounts of its success abound in histories of Revolutionary drama: few fail to mention that the play was performed in nearly every major French city, in front of, by some estimates, over 100,000 spectators,[4] or that it had an initial print run of 20,000 copies, with the Committee of Public Safety funding the purchase of 3,000 copies and the War Ministry ordering 6,000 more to be shipped to the troops.[5] Equally if not more illustrious is the government's decision to provide the Théâtre de la République with twenty pounds each of saltpeter and gunpowder to ensure that every new performance could end with a fake volcanic eruption, at a time when very real wartime shortages threatened the survival of the republic.[6]

No play from the French Revolution, however, is at once so well and so poorly known. Even as they invoke famous examples from its plot or performance history, scholars tend to treat the play as illustrative of something else deemed more significant. For centuries, historians and literary critics presented the play as exhibit A in their case against the theater of the Revolution (and often, against the Revolution itself): "la manifestation la plus répugnante sur la scène des énormités révolutionnaires, du sans-culottisme à l'époque de la Terreur" (the most repugnant manifestation onstage of Revolutionary extravagances, of sans-culottism at the time of the Terror).[7] For these authors, the play's only value lies in its confirmation and illustration of every long-standing (and now largely discredited) preconception about Revolutionary drama: that it was overly topical and political, violent and vulgar, immoral, poorly written, crudely performed, and best forgotten.[8] Even in more recent scholarship, less inclined to sweeping moralistic, aesthetic, and ideological judgments, two near synonyms appear constantly: "refléter" and "représenter" (to reflect and to represent). Maréchal's play "*reflects*" or "*represents*" the militant and satirical theater of the time,[9] the aspirations of the sans-culottes,[10] the symbolism, language, and costumes of the period,[11] or more broadly the mentality,[12] public spirit,[13] and Zeitgeist[14] of the Revolutionaries. Against the impulse to read *The Last Judgment of Kings* as a direct transcription of fixed customs, practices, and ideologies—a remnant, perhaps, of the many years during which Revolutionary theater was viewed almost exclusively as an instrument of propaganda—this critical edition considers it a site of contention, articulating and amplifying the most important debates of the period. The ambition of this volume is thus not only to make this historic play accessible to a broader readership through an annotated French version and an English translation but also to change the ways in which it is read.

Rejecting the tired metaphor of the play as mirror, as something that reflects, I propose that *The Last Judgment of Kings* more closely resembles the best-known feature of Maréchal's play, its volcano: a materialization of hidden conflicts, born of subterranean shifts and clashes, and a figure of ever-accumulating, unstable meanings, as it grows and changes shape with each new layer of molten rock, ash, and gases. *The Last Judgment of Kings* may seem simple, lacking in depth even, yet as in a volcano, most of the activity occurs beneath the surface, where underlying tensions simmer and collide, slowly bubbling upward. Provocative, written in accessible prose, and short—the ideal subject, style, and length to be assigned to students in a French or history seminar—Maréchal's play is a remarkably effective pedagogical tool; it invites its readers to dig into layers upon layers of meaning, less to find a singular truth about the play or the Revolution than to uncover the conflicting forces that gave birth and form to it. In the introduction that follows, I retrace many of these epochal conflicts—about justice, time, religion, commemoration, laughter, and propaganda, among others—and reveal the often unexpected ways that they express themselves in the play. In so doing, I hope to model a response to *The Last Judgment of Kings* that captures what the play meant for its first spectators as well as for the students in my own classes (see the section "A Collaborative Translation"): an opportunity to see tangible illustrations of the most important and contentious questions of the Revolutionary period and to debate them.

A PARODIC IMAGINATION

Before turning to these big thematic questions, some background information on *The Last Judgment of Kings* and its author may prove beneficial, particularly since Maréchal is not solely known today for his volcanic play. Over a long and prolific career that has seen him variously described as a militant atheist, a radical egalitarian, a utopian anarchist, and an agrarian socialist, one other accomplishment stands out as his greatest claim to fame: his creation, one year *before* the Revolution, of a new calendar strikingly similar to the one that would take effect in France in 1793. Entitled *Almanach des honnêtes gens* and among the last books publicly burned by the royal censors of the Ancien Régime, this precursor to the Revolutionary calendar inaugurated ten-day weeks, numerical months, and a new Year One (that of the reign of reason), and replaced Christian saints with philosophers, explorers, writers, and other great men, as well as religious holidays with secular festivals based on the seasons.[15] Along with the almanac's general impiety, the censors specifically decried this parodic element—the repetition of an established form (the calendar) with insertions and substitutions that distorted its accepted meaning and function. In so doing, they singled out an essential aspect of Maréchal's literary strategy. Not only were virtually all of his early works imitations[16] but his 1788 calendar was not even his first blasphemous parody: four years earlier, he had lost a stable position at the Bibliothèque Mazarine by daring to rewrite and lampoon the Bible in *Le Livre échappé au déluge*. Signs of this parodic imagination abound in *The Last Judgment of Kings*. Far from a haphazard aberration born of a disturbed mind or the cultural atrophy of the Terror, as historians and critics argued for centuries, Maréchal's play consists of a carefully constructed literary work that engages in a deliberate dialogue with the practices and ideas of its predecessors. As I will show through a summary of the play, each paratext, each scene, reproduces and subverts conventions, themes, and topoi of its time, weaving a veritable tapestry of citations and reappropriations.

How fitting, therefore, that the first edition of Maréchal's play opens with a self-citation, through which he reveals that the entire play consists of a rewriting of a short parable that he had published a year before the Revolution. In this parable, reproduced exactly and in its entirety from Maréchal's 1788 *Leçons du fils aîné d'un roi*, a madman dreams that all of Earth's peoples rebel simultaneously, seize and try their kings, and sentence them to exile on a secluded but fertile island. Deprived of

their servants, the monarchs reluctantly work the land to survive but soon return to their wicked ways, fighting and exter-
minating one another. The parable's inclusion marks Maréchal
as a prophet (giving more credence to his claim that his play
consists of a "prophecy"), a Revolutionary avant la lettre who
foresaw in 1788 not only the impending popular uprising but also
the later trial and execution of the French monarchs. Yet it
also draws the readers' attention to the changes that Maréchal
introduced between 1788 and 1793, between a succinct text
meant to be read and a longer work meant to be performed.
Not surprisingly, the need to expand the parable leads to the
introduction of several new characters, notably the old man
(whose own banishment by an unjust king serves as a revealing
inversion and foil to the monarchs' exile on the same island),
the savages (who embody the simplicity and goodness of
humankind in its natural state), and the pope (whose deportation alongside the European monarchs adds an anticlerical
dimension to the story). But Maréchal also makes more surprising alterations, not just adding to the parable but trans-
forming its ending as well. The violent brawl through which
the kings destroy one another in the parable becomes a slapstick scuffle in the play, performed in drag and with fake noses,
bawdy gaits, and grimaces. This comedic battle no longer con-
cludes with a moral lesson—the kings' self-destruction, as the
violence of despotism turns against those who once wielded
it—but instead with the eruption of a volcano that engulfs the
ridiculous sovereigns in lava. These are significant changes, to
which we will return in later sections.

The next paratext again engages in an act of self-citation. In
it, Maréchal reproduces a letter that he had published in the
Révolutions de Paris, one of the most widely read and influential newspapers of the Revolutionary period, for which he served
as the principal editor from 1790 to 1794. The letter defends
the "slightly exaggerated" ridicule cast upon the monarchs in
the play by reminding its readers that this merely reverses the

trajectory of laughter in Ancien Régime comedies, which derided and caricatured the people to entertain the royal family and their lackeys. To illustrate his point, Maréchal proceeds to "parody" (his term) a memorable line from the classical comedy *Le Méchant*, modifying a single word—it is no longer "les sots" (fools) but "les rois" (kings) who exist solely, in life and onstage, to elicit merriment—thereby equating fools and kings and inverting the quote's original meaning. In so doing, Maréchal reappropriates not just a famous verse of classical comedy but the latter's general ethos as well, cleverly turning Ancien Régime laughter against itself and its principal beneficiaries (the royal court).[17]

A similar kind of subversive borrowing lies at the center of the next paratext, a remarkably detailed description of the characters' costumes. As Jacques Proust uncovered in an unpublished register preserved in the library of the Comédie-Française, the actors who performed *The Last Judgment of Kings* reused costumes from previous classical plays, in a subtle satire of traditional theater and its repertoire.[18] The slapstick battle in which the rulers of Europe tear their royal garments to pieces thus took on an added signification as the symbolic annihilation not just of the monarchy but also of a particular kind of aristocratic theater, laughter, and culture. By the end of the play, the theatrical tradition that Maréchal and the actors had parroted lay literally in tatters.

The first scene of the play opens on a familiar setting: a secluded island, with a humble hut where a stranded old man resides. For an eighteenth-century audience, this scene would have conjured associations with the many novels and plays in the highly popular Robinsonade tradition. Moreover, Maurice Dommanget notes echoes of a contemporary play by Citoyen Gamas, *Les Emigrés aux terres australes*, and of the better-known *L'Ile des esclaves*, even describing Maréchal's play as "une imitation et une modification de Marivaux" (an imitation and modification of Marivaux).[19] Whether or not Maréchal had a precise source in mind, there is no doubting that the insular setting occupies an especially significant place in the cultural imaginary of the eighteenth century, as Enlightenment philosophers (following the example of Thomas More's *Utopia* and Francis Bacon's *New Atlantis*) treated islands as self-contained laboratories in which to imagine new social and political structures leading to happier, more harmonious communities. If this sounds nothing like the island in *The Last Judgment of Kings*, it is because Maréchal, as was his wont, transforms the topos that he appropriates. Indeed, according to Pawel Matyaszewski, *The Last Judgment of Kings* may be the first example of a new treatment of the island topos as a space of incarceration.[20] The old man, first, and the monarchs, twenty years later, have been banished from society; the island no longer serves as a site where one can create a new, better society but, on the contrary, as the dumping ground for outcasts who threaten the social order beyond the island.

The next scene sees the arrival of the sans-culottes, who explore the island to gauge its suitability as a royal prison. They are thrilled to discover signs of the volcano's imminent eruption (further evidence that the island is a site of punishment, not utopia) and of the presence of a martyr of the Ancien Régime, the old man. Calling out to him at the start of scene III, they lure him out of hiding and ask to hear his story. The ensuing tale constitutes yet another parody, as Maréchal seizes on the opportunity to rewrite a play with a political message antithetical to his own, Charles Collé's *La Partie de chasse de Henri IV*. In this play, written in the early 1760s and wildly popular, both when it was first performed on a public stage in 1774 and during the early years of the Revolution, Henri IV loses his way in a forest, shares a meal incognito with a family of peasants, learns that a virtuous maiden has been kidnapped by a marquis, chastises him publicly, and makes the young woman's marriage to her true love possible by gifting them a rich dowry.[21] The old man's story begins in similar fashion, with a royal hunt that leads the king and his court to violate the privacy of his home. When these gentlemen kidnap the old man's tall, beautiful daughter, however, the king not only fails to intervene, he laughs at the old man and his wife's tearful pleas. Appeals to the queen and to the church fare no better, and by the story's end, the wife is dead from grief and the old man shackled in the hull of a ship, exiled without cause or trial. This darker ending upends the image of the king, from good father (note the dowry) and fount of justice to lascivious and arbitrary tyrant.

It is now the sans-culottes' turn to tell their story, as they attempt to explain the world-shattering event that is the French Revolution to a man who has lived outside of history for the last twenty years. Everything has changed, including language itself, and the sans-culottes find that they must define terms— "guillotine," "sans-culottes," etc.—to bring the old man up to date. This unusual situation, in which a man of the past, of the Ancien Régime, must gradually be eased into the present, may actually have seemed quite familiar to many in the audience, for it had already been used in several plays during the early years of the Revolution, most notably in Claude-Marie-Louis-Emmanuel Carbon de Flins Des Oliviers's popular *Le Réveil d'Épiménide à Paris*, in which a man falls asleep during the reign of Louis XIV, wakes up one hundred years later in 1790, and sets out to understand the new world around him.[22] Yet Maréchal tweaks this topos, as his sans-culottes not only guide the old man to the spectators' present (October 1793) but push further ahead into their supposed future, describing the uprising of the other peoples of Europe and the trial, conviction, and exile of their kings. He thus combines two distinct iterations of the time-traveling sleeper: on the one hand, Carbon de Flins Des Oliviers's Epimenides (and, later, Washington Irving's Rip Van Winkle), and on the other, Louis-Sébastien Mercier's nameless slumberer in one of the bestsellers of the eighteenth century, *L'An 2440, rêve s'il en fut jamais*.[23] The former falls asleep in the past and wakes up in the present; the latter nods off in the present and awakens in the future. This enables Maréchal to draw on the advantages presented by both iterations: disparaging the past and extolling the present through the first kind of sleeper, and prophesizing an even better future, a uchronia, through the second.

Next come the savages, another recurrent figure in the eighteenth-century imaginary. They first appear onstage at the end of scene III, but their role in the play is best captured in the line that, alone, comprises the entirety of scene IV: "Braves sans-culottes, ces sauvages sont nos aînés en liberté: car ils n'ont jamais eu de rois. Nés libres, ils vivent et meurent comme ils sont nés" (Brave sans-culottes, these savages are our elders in liberty as they have never had a king. Born free, they live and die as they were born).[24] As suggested by the likely allusion to one of Jean-Jacques Rousseau's best-known aphorisms—"L'homme est né libre, et partout il est dans les fers" (Man is born free, and everywhere he is in chains)[25]—the savages appear to be perfect illustrations of the myth of the noble savage commonly (if somewhat unfairly) associated with Rousseau in the eighteenth century. Untainted by civilization, they retain humanity's intrinsic goodness, freedom, and simplicity, bringing fruit, game, and fish to the old man every evening for twenty years and fraternizing instantly with the sans-culottes. Strikingly, however, Maréchal passes on the opportunity to write a "reverse ethnography" in the style of Michel de Montaigne's "Des Cannibales" or Denis Diderot's "Supplément au voyage de Bougainville." Although the list of costumes printed before the play states that one savage has a speaking part, none of the indigenous people ever utters a word and they never, therefore, offer an outsider's perspective on Western society. Nor does the play convey any substantive information about the savages' lifestyle and mores that might serve as a contrast and indirect critique of their European visitors. However blissful and virtuous the savages' ignorance, nothing in the play suggests that the sans-culottes should seek to return to a more natural state by imitating or joining them (in fact, the old man spends twenty years alone on his volcanic island instead of integrating with their nearby community).

Yet if the savages do not function in Maréchal's play as noble foils to an inferior West, at least not as directly as one might have anticipated, neither do they play the opposite role sometimes assigned to indigenous people, particularly in stranded white men narratives: as illustrations of the superiority of Western culture. In the Robinsonade tradition, the marooned Europeans tame a hostile nature and acculturate backward savages to Western mores as steps on the path toward rebuilding civilization. By contrast, in *The Last Judgment of Kings*, the old man refuses to serve as the savages' sovereign and makes them promise instead that they will never again seek to be ruled, be it by kings or by priests. This symbolic gesture, through which the old man declines to be an agent of so-called progress or civilization, replicates the decision by another wise elder in Montesquieu's famous parable of the Troglodytes, who had likewise turned down a crown to keep his friends and neighbors from entering civil society and abandoning a life of inner virtue and free will for one of external laws and discipline.[26] In the end, neither the savages nor the Europeans seem transformed in any meaningful way from having come into contact with the other. On the contrary, the lessons enclosed in the old man's story preserve the savages in their natural state outside history, which no doubt explains why they simply vanish from the play as soon as they have fulfilled their role as indignant witnesses to the procession of kings in the next scene. This is, in fact, the savages' principal function in the play: as we will see, their mute but symbolic presence opposite the kings enables Maréchal to assemble a triptych onstage, with the ahistorical savages and the degenerate monarchs embodying the two extremes of humanity and delimiting a middle ground for the sans-culottes to occupy.

The procession of kings, one of the most memorable moments in the play, takes up the entirety of scene V. The way it unfolds clearly mimics legal proceedings. The kings are brought forward one by one, in chains as in a tribunal, with the savages and the old man for an audience. Each monarch faces a sans-culotte judge from his or her nation who levels detailed and carefully constructed accusations pertaining to specific crimes (with a few exceptions: the Spanish king for instance is only accused of having the facial features of a Bourbon!). Each king is given the opportunity to respond publicly to these charges, after which they receive individual sentences from their judge. Other elements, however, would have no place in a courtroom. The kings' shackles encircle their necks, and each chain is held by a sans-culotte, who drags the monarch behind him like a master walks a pet. This analogy struck Maréchal's contemporaries; no fewer than four likened the procession of kings to the parading of bears and other dancing beasts during fairground spectacles.[27] The sensation of having been transported to a fair or carnival was further amplified by the kings' costumes and acting style, not only the aspects clearly borrowed from popular genres like farce (fake noses and posteriors, lewd gestures, and over-the-top pantomime) but also the way that the play co-opted and ridiculed the most sacred symbols, as when Catherine II and the pope used their imperial scepter and holy cross as batons in a slapstick duel. Maréchal thus took one of the most solemn rituals, a trial—and not just any trial but that of kings, a repetition of the recent, epoch-defining proceedings against Louis XVI and Marie-Antoinette—and flipped it upside down into one of the least solemn spectacles, a fairground farce.

The kings' arrival onstage prompts, in fact, a radical shift in the tone of the play and in Maréchal's use of parody. In the first four scenes, the play had focused on extolling the virtues of the old man, the sans-culottes, the savages, and the Revolution. Accordingly, its tone was serious to the point of grandiloquence, with no attempt at levity or comedy, and when Maréchal parodied a topos or stock character—the island setting, the time-traveling sleeper, the noble savages—it was to repurpose and tweak it but not ridicule it. Once the kings disembark, however, and for the rest of the play's second half, Maréchal no longer employs parody as a mode of rewriting but as one of comic inversion. Repetition of the sort does not add or expand, it diminishes; it targets all that is high, sacred, and distinguished, and brings it low.

Examples of this parodic inversion abound in scene VI. At the end of the burlesque trial, the sans-culottes abandon their former sovereigns on the island, after calling (prophetically) on nature to incinerate them with its fiery breath. The kings, now alone, ponder how to survive, their avowed aversion to the most obvious answer—manual labor—leading the Spanish king to suggest cannibalism instead. In addition to highlighting the kings' laziness, this proposal recalls an earlier passage during the kings' trial, when the French sans-culotte had condemned them as follows: "C'était pour procurer des jouissances à ces mangeurs d'hommes, que le peuple, du matin au soir, et d'un bout de l'année à l'autre, travaillait, suait, s'épuisait" (It was to provide amusements to these man-eaters that the people, from dawn to dusk, and from the start of the year to its end, worked, sweated, and exhausted themselves).[28] These two passages set up an opposition between the common people, who produce their own food, and monarchs, who depend on others for sustenance, devouring not only the fruits of their servants' labor but even more shockingly their bodies as well. Maréchal chooses this accusation not just for its shock value but also because it inverts one of the most common slurs against the sans-culottes, whose supposed cannibalism inspired countless legends and satirical engravings among opponents of the Revolution.[29] As early as the play's first paragraph, in fact, Maréchal ridicules the belief that humanity, without the restraints of civilization and high culture, regresses into anthropophagic barbarity, by having the old man observe that while the people of his country would have expected the savages to feast upon him like cannibals, they had instead nourished him for twenty years.

Similarly, the wealthy, outwardly civilized counterrevolution-aries leveled accusations of cannibalism against those poorer and less cultivated than them, when they were the ones who for centuries had sucked the people's blood and sweat like leeches. By reclaiming the word cannibal, Maréchal thus not only parodies the language of the elite, he turns it against them, exposing their own parasitic reliance on the bodies of others.

The remaining scenes of the play confirm this, as the royal parasites, starved of subjects, increasingly prey on one another, until they lose all humanity and are reduced to mere bodies. Catherine II challenges the pope to a duel, or rather, to a travesty of a tragic duel, wielding her scepter like a sword and shattering the holy man's cross before forcing him to confess that he is nothing more than a charlatan, a fairground prestidigitator. No sooner has peace returned than the monarchs discover that the Spanish king has retained a morsel of rye bread and engage in a mass brawl to steal it. When the compassionate sans-culottes suspend the melee by giving the kings a barrel of crackers, the monarchs once again begin to quarrel, their argument over how to divide the crackers parodying in explicit terms the wars they once waged to partition Europe (such as the Silesian Wars). These momentous conflicts that cost the lives of hundreds of thousands of men, women, and children appear ridiculous over a barrel of crackers, as ridiculous as the rulers themselves when they fence with scepter and cross like two Guignols with their sticks or when they resort to hilarious fist-icuffs and rip their extravagant costumes to shreds for a scrap of bread. Such comedic battles in the style of a popular carnival or farce strip the kings (literally) of their superficial superiority and reveal underneath their monstrous bodies, just as the same process of inversion elevates the simple sans-culottes who are so far from cannibals that even in a position of strength they continue to feed the kings who once fed on them.

The kings do not quarrel for long, as they are interrupted in the eighth and final scene by the volcano's eruption. It is tempting to regard this memorable ending as entirely original: it does not appear in the parable, nor, to my knowledge, does it parody a similar staged explosion in an earlier play (it did, however, inspire several imitations, notably Hippolyte Pellet-Desbarreaux's *Les Potentats foudroyés par la Montagne et la Raison, ou la Déportation des Rois de l'Europe, pièce prophétique et révolutionnaire*).[30] Yet the volcano is in reality the most polysemic element of the entire play, as multilayered and unstable as an actual volcano. Not only does Maréchal's volcano take on different meanings depending on the framework—judicial, temporal, religious, commemorative, artistic, or political—in which it is positioned, but even within each of these frameworks it remains a malleable figure that supports antithetical interpretations. Is the volcano a symbol of:

1) The violence of the Terror or its repudiation?

2) The Revolution as unprecedented rupture or as cyclical regeneration?

3) Secularization or a new civic religion?

4) Revolutionary festivals as sites of memory or erasure?

5) Popular laughter or republican solemnity?

6) Political propaganda or abstract virtue?

As contradictory as it may seem, the answer is all of the above. Embracing such polysemy as one of the play's principal virtues, the rest of this introduction is structured around the volcano, with each section exploring the ways in which it was perceived by Maréchal's contemporaries, how it has since been interpreted by scholars, and to what extent these interpretations reflect and expand on pivotal debates in the historiography of the Revolution. Using the volcano as both a starting point and a through line, the six thematic sections below thus offer different entryways into the culture and history of the French

Revolution and the fundamental questions that it raised, at the time and still to this day.

VOLCANIC JUSTICE

Incredibly, given the clarity of the historical record and the significance of the play, considerable confusion remains about the exact date of its premiere. According to thirteen scholars, the sovereigns in Maréchal's play first met their spectacular and untimely end at the Théâtre de la République on October 17, 1793, just one day after Marie-Antoinette had her own star turn on the scaffold.[31] But for twelve others, among them some of today's most prominent specialists of eighteenth-century theater, the premiere of *The Last Judgment of Kings* occurred a day later, on October 18.[32] Uncertainty even strikes within individual texts, as when Régine Jomand-Baudry, in an article, and Emmet Kennedy, in the most reliable repertory of scenic productions during the French Revolution, offer fluctuating dates— sometimes the seventeenth, sometimes the eighteenth—for the premiere.[33] Whatever the source of this confusion,[34] it is itself confusing, as newspaper reports from the period make it unambiguously clear that the premiere took place on the seventeenth, not the eighteenth (although the play was also performed that evening).[35] This makes the play's juxtaposition with the death of Marie-Antoinette just twenty-four hours earlier all the more inescapable, not only for scholars but for the play's first spectators as well. Indeed, it is entirely conceivable that some of the audience members cheering as the volcano's fire engulfed the European kings onstage had acclaimed the thud of the guillotine's blade on the Austrian queen's neck just a day prior.

The play encourages this parallel as early as the second scene, when the English sans-culotte, rejoicing that the island has an active volcano, predicts that "la main de la nature s'empressera de ratifier, de sanctionner le jugement porté par les sans-culottes contre les rois" (Nature, by her own hands, will soon ratify and sanction the sans-culottes' judgment against the kings).[36]

In fact, the volcanic eruption at the end of the play provides a symbolic resolution to not just one but three trials, which repeat and mimic one another. As stated in the quote above, it legitimizes the trial of the European monarchs, which, we are told by the English sans-culotte, took place before the start of the play when the peoples of Europe rebelled and formally tried their kings, sentencing them to exile. But as the play makes clear, this trial was itself inspired by the example given by the French when they judged Louis XVI and Marie-Antoinette.[37] Considering the recency of Marie-Antoinette's execution and the intensity of the dissensions and emotional reactions provoked by Louis XVI's trial—already described by Maréchal, at the time, as "le jugement dernier" (the last judgment)[38]—it stands to reason that the spectators of the play would have perceived the imaginary trial and death of European monarchs as a repetition of the very real trial and death of their own former sovereigns.[39] This seems all the more probable given that the spectators were presented, within the play, with a second repetition of their former monarchs' trial—a repetition of a repetition—when the sans-culottes, tasked only with executing the verdict of the European convention by dumping the kings on a secluded island, inexplicably decide to hold a parodic trial that judges anew the already convicted kings. Indeed, as we noted earlier, the procession of fallen monarchs in scene V looks strikingly like legal proceedings, as each shackled ruler is confronted with a sans-culotte judge of the same nationality, leading to detailed, targeted accusations and, after the kings have been given a chance to respond to these charges, individual sentences from their own personal judge.

Through this scene, the play does not simply narrate a trial (that of the European kings) or allude to one (the proceedings against Louis XVI and Marie-Antoinette); it becomes itself a judicial act. The idea that kings ought to be tried appears in many of Maréchal's works, including, of course, the 1788 parable that Maréchal reproduces as a paratext to the play. Yet

The Last Judgment of Kings differs from the parable in important ways: it takes a short, written declaration of broad antimonarchical sentiment and turns it into a series of specific accusations against real kings, embodied onstage. It draws on the unique attributes of the theater—agonistic debate, live presence, an actively judging audience—that make it the closest art form to legal proceedings, a likeness that Maréchal had already sought to exploit in early 1793 by proposing a new type of performance: "je conseillerais [au public] de faire comparaître devant lui, sur la scène, à tout le moins une fois l'an, ses rois ou ses magistrats, et de les juger avec la même impartialité qu'il juge un poète, un acteur ou un virtuose" (I would advise the public to make its kings or magistrates appear before it onstage at least once a year and to judge them with the same impartiality with which it judges a poet, an actor, or a virtuoso).[40] *The Last Judgment of Kings* comes close to realizing this vision and perfectly illustrates the progression toward a "judicial theater" that I trace in my book *Dramatic Justice: Trial by Theater in the Age of the French Revolution.*[41] Like many other plays from the late eighteenth century, it transforms the theater into a tribunal by reenacting contemporary crimes and inviting its spectators to pass judgment on real-life figures.

In fact, Maréchal's play is not only a trial—the European kings'—it is also the trial of a trial, insofar as it allowed audience members to reexperience and voice their opinions on the recent proceedings against their own monarchs. Writing for the *Révolutions de Paris*, Maréchal had complained throughout Louis XVI's trial about the delays caused by the Girondins' insistence on respecting legal forms that should never have applied to a clearly guilty tyrant.[42] *The Last Judgment of Kings* represented an opportunity to stage the trial as it should have unfolded, without formalities and plodding esoteric debates: just a direct interrogation, a prompt verdict, and a swift execution. Yet this makes it even more peculiar that the sans-culottes abandon the sovereigns on the secluded island instead of immediately killing them. Banishment had, after all, been the preferred sentence of many Girondins during Louis XVI's trial, much to Maréchal's and the Montagnards' dismay.[43] When the old man draws attention to this incongruity by noting that hanging the kings would have been more expedient than deporting them, the sans-culottes offer several explanations: such a punishment would have been far too swift for kings who first had to suffer for their crimes;[44] it would have bloodied the hands of the good sans-culottes;[45] and it would have lacked the moral lesson imparted by the inevitable outcome of the sovereigns' insular incarceration, the moment when they turned on one another and died by their own hands.[46] Maréchal's parable had ended precisely in this way, with the miserable tyrants responsible for their own extinction.[47] But then why change the play's ending by adding a volcanic eruption? Because of this addition, differing judgments saturate the play—the judgment of the sans-culotte convention (exile), the judgment of nature (death by lava), the judgment of the audience (derisive laughter)—revealing the existence of conflicting emotions about Revolutionary justice and punishment.

As the sans-culottes explain to the old man, the first sentence—exile—derives from a conception of justice as spectacle: as a morality tale centered on the public display of guilt and suffering. This vision underpins the Girondin argument that Louis XVI had to be formally tried (against the wishes of the Montagnards who wanted him summarily executed) because a trial would make his crimes public. It also explains why so many voted for his exile (effective once the war had ended), with Thomas Paine proposing the United States as one destination where Louis and his family would learn to love representative democracy.[48] This sentimental narrative of redemption and social rehabilitation was commonplace in the early years of the Revolution, with plays like *Les Émigrés aux terres australes* showing exile's potential to enlighten aristocrats to the merits of a new, reformed society.[49] Yet while it also appears to motivate the kings' banishment in the 1788 parable, with Maréchal stressing that the island is fertile and that the deposed monarchs would learn the value of work in order to survive, the ending, with the kings returning to their old ways and tearing each other to pieces, undercuts the very sentimental narrative the parable had initially invoked. The play further undermines it through a counternarrative: the old man was banished to the exact same island, but nature and the savages recognized his innocence and purity, and he survived for twenty years where the kings fail to last a day. Even after being shown compassion in the form of a barrel of crackers, the like of which was never offered to the old man, the monarchs never reflect on their guilt (their only regret is having been too soft on their subjects) and repeat instead the very crimes of which they have been accused, waging war on one another instead of dividing the barrel equitably. Exile does not reform character traits; it reveals them. Indeed, there is never any hope of redemption for the kings in the play: the sole purpose of deportation is to offer Europe "le spectacle de ses tyrans détenus dans une ménagerie et se dévorant les uns les autres" (the spectacle of its tyrants held in a menagerie, devouring each other).[50] Punishment remains a spectacle but a tragic rather than a sentimental one, with characters whose fate is sealed by their own irredeemable flaws. Such a spectacle imbues justice with a clear moral lesson: the very crimes perpetrated by the kings—the exile of the old man— are now visited upon them, but rather than learn from this they respond with further greed and violence, becoming the instruments of their own downfall.

The volcano, described earlier as the hand of Nature, enacts a different kind of justice, swifter and more immanent than its human counterpart.[51] Scholars from Jean-Marie Apostolidès to Mary Ashburn Miller have argued that the volcano exemplifies the Montagnard conception of justice that came to the fore during the King's trial and inspired the Reign of Terror.[52] Nature, through the volcano, must intervene (unlike in the parable, written in a different era) because kings are no longer perceived as flawed humans but as "monsters" existing beyond the jurisdiction of positive law. The play's rhetoric—the way that kings are portrayed as intrinsically nonhuman—and its foregrounding of the kings' grotesque, libidinous, and violent bodies have the same function in the play as they did in Louis's and Marie-Antoinette's trials: to publicly demonstrate the monarchs' monstrosity, which justifies prosecuting them less for having committed a particular infraction against positive law than simply for existing, like monsters, in violation of natural law. Human laws and tribunals do not apply to creatures who have alienated themselves from the social contract and from humanity writ large; their death is not an act of human justice but a swift, purificatory elimination by nature itself. In this reading, the volcanic eruption signals Maréchal's support for the paring down and acceleration of legal proceedings during the Terror (with the trials of the Revolutionary Tribunal increasingly frequent, summary, and lethal due to restrictions on defense attorneys and witnesses as well as the practice of bundling large groups of defendants and reaching a single verdict—death or innocence—for all). The volcano stands for the Mountain (a widespread analogy, even prior to the play): both inflict punishments that are swift, infallible enactments of natural law, slaying monsters (kings, aristocrats, priests, and traitors) while sparing true patriots.[53] This parallel explains why for centuries the play and, above all, its volcanic climax have been viewed as an endorsement of terrorist violence, a declaration by the Mountain that when it kills, it does so legitimately and naturally, like a volcano.

Yet if the volcano has often been interpreted as a manifestation of terror, it may not have been perceived as such by contemporary audiences. Scholars like to cite the *Feuille du salut public* article in which Alexandre Rousselin memorably describes the spectators as transformed by the play into a "légion de tyrannicides, prêts à s'élancer sur l'espèce *léonine*, connue sous le nom de rois" (legion of tyrannicides, poised to throw themselves upon the leonine species known as kings).[54] But most other reviews of the play focus instead on the laughter it elicited, and indeed there can be little doubt that this was the response sought by Maréchal.[55] When the monarchs see the volcano erupt, they do not scream or cry or react in such a way as to stir in the spectators a parallel response of terror and awe before the sheer force of nature; no, they invite laughter with ridiculous promises by the pope to take a wife and by Catherine II to join a Revolutionary club if they survive. The spectators could be forgiven if they saw in the volcano less an imposing substitute for the Mountain than the finale to many carnivals: a balloon throwing out flames to represent hell.[56] Likewise, the mass brawl over the barrel of crackers could have unfolded in *Lord of the Flies* style, as it does in the more serious parable where the kings viciously destroy one another, but instead, the spectators were treated to a comedic melee which, reviews tell us, was staged with all the trappings of the carnival: cross-dressing, fake noses and other prosthetics, bawdy gaits and grimaces, and the most elevated figures, an empress and a pope, fencing with scepter and cross like two Guignols with their sticks.[57] In the transition from page to stage, Maréchal opts for a different destruction of the kings, not through terrifying violence but through derision. As he makes clear in the letter first published in the *Révolutions de Paris* and then repurposed as a preface to the play, *The Last Judgment of Kings* aims to turn the monarchs into laughingstocks in retribution for the centuries that they dared laugh at the sovereign people.

This third judgment differs from the previous two, as it appears less a mise en abyme of Revolutionary justice than a response to its violence. Of course, derision carries its own violence—notably as a weapon against the sacrality of kings—but one that remains symbolic and pales in comparison to the very real violence committed against the queen's body the night before. When the play repeats the queen's execution as a carnivalesque parody, what is the intended impact on the audience? The volcano takes the place of the guillotine, which could be seen as praising it by presenting it as natural, but which also erases it, as if it were a source of guilt. Someone has to operate the guillotine, but the volcano kills without the need for human agents, absolving the sans-culottes and the National Convention of any responsibility for the violent deaths they inflicted on the French monarchs and many others. Whereas in real life the Revolutionaries soiled their hands with the blood of a king and queen still revered by many French people as sacred or parental figures, onstage the sans-culottes refrain from direct violence (quite the opposite: they offer food out of compassion) and let nature determine their prisoners' fate.[58] A similar desire to defuse the violence of the Revolution might also explain Maréchal's turn to comedy: hence, for Pierre Frantz, "la violence réelle, si fortement symbolique et transgressive dans les mentalités, exigeait une sorte de réitération innocente, tolérable et joyeuse" (real violence, so deeply symbolic and transgressive in the mindset of the time, demanded a kind of innocent, tolerable, and joyous reiteration).[59] In laughter, the spectators could find not only absolution but also a form of "decompression."[60] Therein resided the appeal of the exaggerated humor of the carnival, from the farcical brawls to the dummy volcano, which could reassure the spectators that the events onstage were not real and that they could thus safely laugh at their violence. Guillaume Cot even proposes that laughing at the violence onstage could reveal to the spectators the possibility of its coming to an end outside the theater, so that the volcano's eruption served, unexpectedly, as "le coup de canon final de la violence révolutionnaire" (the final cannon shot of Revolutionary violence).[61] This is a far cry from the traditional portrayal of *The Last Judgment of Kings* as an endorsement of the Terror and of Revolutionary bloodshed. Such ambiguity, however, is precisely what makes the play such a great window into the Revolution's complex relationship to justice and punishment.

TIME IS A VOLCANO

In the eighteenth century, volcanoes stood as a symbol of time, but crucially not always the same concept of time. On the one hand, as Sanja Perovic and David McCallam have shown, volcanoes may have served as the period's quintessential image of rupture, with each eruption perceived as an irreversible break in time.[62] Such is the power of a volcano's eruption that it destroys everything in its path, erasing the past entirely and clearing the ground for a new beginning unlike anything that preceded it. It creates a before and an after, a sudden caesura that alters the course of history. On the other hand, the volcano belongs to a natural, geological time that unfolds cyclically, not linearly. Its eruptions are periodic, and ever since the discoveries of Pompeii and Herculaneum (about which Maréchal wrote nine volumes), all marveled at the ability of volcanoes not just to erase the past but to freeze it, allowing it to be revived in the present and fixed there forever.[63] As a symbol of time, the volcano thus manifests the same ambiguity as the term "revolution," which by the end of the eighteenth century combined the astronomical sense of a cyclical return to a known past with the more recent meaning of a radical historical rupture leading to a new and unprecedented present. These two contradictory concepts of time at the core of both the volcano and the term "revolution" come to a particularly revealing clash in *The Last Judgment of Kings*. Given that one of Maréchal's principal claims to fame lay in his authorship of the first attempt at a Revolutionary calendar, it is hardly surprising that he understood better than most that defining the temporality of the Revolution amounted to determining its meaning, as well as when and how it would end.[64] Was the French Revolution a moral and political regeneration—a cyclical return to a more natural golden age or to Greco-Roman antiquity—or a rupture in time that set France on a new path of irreversible, linear progress?

This hesitation between two concepts of time characterizes the play's uniquely complex temporal structure, always looking backward and forward at once. Scene III is a perfect example of this. Confronted with an old man who, for twenty years, has lived outside of history, the sans-culottes set out to resynchronize him by teaching him about the key dates, symbols, and figures of the Revolution. This provides Maréchal with an ideal opportunity to revive and praise the recent past of the spectators. But the sans-culottes then begin to narrate events that transpired after 1793. In that moment, they are resynchronizing not only the old man but the spectators as well, revealing to them their own victorious future.[65] Indeed, as Apostolidès explains, the prophecy in the title is as much about legitimizing the past as it is about imagining the future. The play encourages its spectators to project themselves into a future that repeats their recent past (the trial and executions of the king and queen, the dechristianization campaign, etc.) because this will allow them to see their own actions as later generations would: as just and necessary steps in a triumphant history.[66] Even as the play collapses past and future into a prophecy of continuous linear progress, however, it also adds to the initial parable evocations of a golden age of savages and sun cults, further muddying the water about the temporality—rupture or regeneration—of the Revolution.

According to Perovic, Maréchal was "the first writer to explicitly formulate the novelty of the Revolution as a 'rupture in time' and thus as a new mode of historical action."[67] First or not, Maréchal offers in *The Last Judgment of Kings* a uniquely vivid dramatization of the concept of revolution as rupture when the old man struggles to comprehend the language ("guillotiner," "sans-culotte") used by those on the other side of the temporal caesura. Indeed, in the story told to the old man by the sans-culottes, the French Revolution is not the culmination of a gradual process of emancipation but an instantaneous eruption of the popular will: "Le peuple français s'est levé. Il a dit: *je ne veux plus de roi*; et le trône a disparu. Il a dit encore: *je veux la république*, et nous voilà tous républicains" (The people of France rose up. They said, *We no longer want a king.* And the throne disappeared. They then said, *We want a republic*, and here we all are, republicans).[68] Years of violence and vacillation are elided into a single foundational moment when the will of the people transformed history by entering it, as suddenly and irrevocably as a volcanic eruption.[69] This rupture fractures the cyclical time of the monarchy ("the king is dead, long live the king") and replaces it with the linear time of republican progress. Thereafter, time follows a fixed historical path, one that is universal and teleological. Hence, the other European nations not only rise up, instantaneously and simultaneously like the French, they also follow the exact same historical progression, as if no other could possibly exist: "En effet, une insurrection générale et simultanée a éclaté chez toutes les nations de l'Europe; et chacune d'elles eut son 14 juillet et 5 octobre 1789, son 10 août et 21 septembre 1792, son 31 mai et 2 juin 1793" (Indeed, a general, simultaneous insurrection burst forth in all the nations of Europe, and they each had their own 14th of July and 5th of October 1789, their own 10th of August and 21st of September 1792, their own May 31st and June 2nd of 1793). The Revolution's rupture in time causes national histories and differences to collapse into a singular world History, of which it is the start. Every subsequent event must follow the same script, retracing the path from tyranny to freedom: to question this teleological vision of history would mean to question the legitimacy of the Revolution itself. It is in fact indicative of the popularity of this concept of time that many spectators accepted at face value Maréchal's highly unusual designation of his play as a "prophecy."[70] Far from the reveries of a "madman," as they were depicted in the parable, the events in Maréchal's play were treated in newspaper reports of the time as soon-to-be historical facts, the logical, inevitable next step in the Revolution's linear progress.[71]

In such a forward-looking play, one wonders what need there is of primitive savages, yet Maréchal must have had a reason to add them to the plot of his parable. As we saw earlier, these savages, uncorrupted by civilization, are naturally innocent and kind. On three occasions Maréchal specifies that they arrive on the island in familial groups (unlike the kings, who appear onstage individually), suggesting a lack of differentiation and hierarchies that is further highlighted in the list of characters, where they are described as being "de tout âge et de tout sexe" (of all ages and sexes).[72] Having never known a king, living in the simplest and most natural social structure—the family—they incarnate freedom and equality. This explains their instant harmony with the sans-culottes ("on fraternise; on s'embrasse" [they fraternize; they embrace]) and their ability to communicate with the old man through gestures, since "le cœur est de tous les pays" (the heart is of all countries).[73] Pantomime, the original, natural language of humanity according to Rousseau, Diderot, and other eighteenth-century thinkers, can thus collapse temporal and cultural difference and bring together individuals that articulated speech separates, but only for those whose hearts have retained their natural goodness.[74]

The addition of the savages and their association with an idealized nature points toward a conception of revolution as regeneration and of time as cyclical. It should be noted however that Maréchal is not advocating a simplistic return to a state of nature. The sans-culottes and the old man never even consider living with the savages instead of returning to Europe. Rather, the savages and the kings serve to illustrate the two extremes of humanity—in a text written just months before *The Last Judgment of Kings*, Maréchal describes the former as "*pas encore* l'homme" (not yet human) and "l'homme informe" (the unformed human), and the latter as "*plus* l'homme" (no longer human) and "l'homme déformé" (the deformed human)—so as to reveal the existence of a middle ground, the golden age that the Revolution must revive.[75] In this golden age, human beings lived in self-sufficient, patriarchal family units subsisting through agrarian labor. There existed neither masters nor servants, neither kings nor subjects, neither rich nor poor; the only laws were those made by benevolent fathers for the good of their grateful progeny.[76] The chasm between this golden age and the society birthed by the Revolution explains why throughout the early 1790s Maréchal repeatedly sided, in one of the period's most significant debates, with those who saw the Revolution as unfinished.[77] While praising its role in destroying age-old prejudices, Maréchal lamented that the Revolution had effected superficial changes in costume and speech but stopped short of challenging social, political, and economic inequalities. The Revolutionaries' embrace of a social contract and their institution of a democracy had merely created new hierarchies of wealth and power, no more natural or justifiable than those in other political regimes. Finishing the Revolution would require recognizing the impurity of any and all civil society and returning instead to the golden age of small, self-governing families.

The problem with this cyclical conception of the Revolution lies in the possible return not only of the golden age but also of its subsequent degeneration into monarchy. Maréchal often recounts the same standard political history in his writings which explains how small families, misled by their instinct of sociability and by the deceptive structural analogy between a father leading a family and a king leading his people, come to freely choose a sovereign and enter civil society.[78] A similar tale seems about to unfold in *The Last Judgment of Kings* when the families of savages, whose insularity has spared them any knowledge of tyranny, attempt to crown the old man as king. Yet the story ends differently, because the old man has firsthand experience of the ways that monarchies supplant and destroy the natural family structure, a king having kidnapped his daughter, caused the death of his wife, and exiled him. The old man shares his painfully acquired wisdom with the savages and makes them promise never to allow a king or priest on their island. Interestingly, he accepts the status of father even as he rejects that of king, thereby severing the two roles and preserving the savages' natural view of fatherhood from contamination by the monarchy. Having experienced both civilization (in France) and nature (on the island), the old man possesses the foresight to stop the savages' degeneration, to guide them, as a father, to the golden age and then keep them there, frozen in time before the fall.

The old man's suspension of cyclical political history illustrates the best way to finish the Revolution for Maréchal. In his *Correctif à la Révolution*, he explains that it was necessary for Europeans to experience civil society at its worst, like the old man did, in order to develop not only the desire to return to a primitive golden age but also the wisdom to remain there forever.[79] The Revolutionaries must enact a familial, agrarian system that is modeled on an age of blissful, virtuous innocence but that is not so innocent that it simply repeats the past without introducing the changes and safeguards made necessary by the harsh lessons of history; in other words, the Revolutionaries must find a way to cycle back and yet break the cycle. What is needed is what the play's title promises: a Last Judgment, that is, the moment that time itself comes to an end. Susan McCready and Proust both underline the religious conception of time that the image of a Last Judgment evokes. McCready notes that the volcanic eruption that fulfills the Last Judgment destroys not only the tyrants but also the old man's calendar, drawn onto a large rock, through which he had, for the past twenty years, clung onto time amid a sea of sameness. Its destruction marks a new beginning, "in which time itself is transformed into infinity."[80] Likewise, Proust argues that for Maréchal, the Revolution is a revelation, a transition from secular history into the fixed, ahistorical time of the sacred.[81] Once finished, the Revolution will be at once cyclical (the return of an earlier golden age) and a rupture (the end of time, of history, to ensure that this cycle is, like the judgment, the last).

Maréchal thus succeeds—if only through a fiction—in reconciling the two conflicting notions of time as rupture and as regeneration.[82]

THE ATHEIST VOLCANO AND THE SUN CULT

This religious conception of time may seem at odds with Maréchal's reputation as one of France's first openly militant atheists. Yet in its treatment of religion, as in everything else, *The Last Judgment of Kings* proves surprisingly complex. Once again, the volcano looms over the issue as it is, until the old man's arrival, the sole religious object in the play, with the savages coming every day at dusk to worship it. The savages' nightly ritual recalls another ceremony described in Maréchal's writings: that of the Ausones, an ancient tribe who saw in Mount Vesuvius the wrath of their god, the sun, and who set out to appease it periodically by casting into the burning crater expiatory victims, chosen on the basis of the threat their ambition posed to the tribe's primitive equality.[83] It also brings to mind the topos of the last judgment of kings found in many medieval texts, which often shows monarchs in the fires of hell as a warning that all human beings, no matter their station, ultimately face God's judgment.[84] In both instances the volcano punishes in the name of equality, as it does in the play, sparing those who worship it and eradicating the despots who dared believe themselves superior to the rest of humanity. Maréchal adds another, more anticlerical dimension to the story, however, by adding the pope to the list of victims (unlike in his original parable, where only kings had been deported). Paradoxically, the volcano thus becomes at once an object of religious worship and, to quote McCallam, "an active agent of atheist Revolution" tasked with destroying the false religion of Catholicism.[85] Its obliteration of the pope echoes and sanctions the religious vandalism happening at the same time as the play's premiere, whether it was the disinterring and desecration of the cadavers of French kings and queens in the Basilica of Saint-Denis or the replacement of religious symbols, statues, and crosses with busts of Marat and Lepelletier in churches throughout France.[86]

Indeed, much suggests, beyond just the pope's violent end, that Maréchal's play belongs to the dechristianization campaign that reached its climax in the second half of 1793. *The Last Judgment of Kings* puts on a theatrical stage many of the standard attributes of the vast, open-air festivals held in the fall and winter of 1793 to weaken Catholicism, such as the parodic procession of deposed rulers, their mock trials, and their fiery executions (often via the burning of effigies).[87] Also found in both the play and the dechristianization festivals: a deep attention to costume and ornament as instruments of desacralization (hence the remarkably detailed descriptions of the characters' costumes in the preface to the play). Holy figures like divine-right monarchs and popes wear lavish clothing that, as in a caricature, draws from reality but exaggerates it to the point of grotesqueness. This sensation is heightened by the addition of adornments from the very opposite (much lower) sphere—fake noses and prosthetics, chains worn as leashes, and a papal cross that prior to the Revolution could never have been shown onstage to preserve its sacrality, now turned into a Guignol's baton and shattered into pieces. By the end of the play, the kings and the pope have torn their costumes to shreds, destroying the symbols of their professed holiness and disclosing beneath these empty signs the frail, flawed bodies of earthly creatures. Where better to strip the church of a sacrality accrued through superficial rituals, costumes, and artifices than the theater, the site of a perpetual play between seeming and being, illusion and reality?

Yet just as the volcano both supports and undercuts religion in the play, Maréchal's *Last Judgment of Kings* goes beyond the purely destructive dimension of dechristianization. When the old man learns of the savages' vespertine volcanic cult, he does not mock or oppose it but instead supplements it by teaching them to worship the rising sun as well. This embrace of religion in a play by a militant atheist like Maréchal may seem perplexing, but even the most fervent devotees of dechristianization understood the need to offer the people something to believe in. The same factions, notably the Hébertists, who strove to erase all traces of Christianity, also called for their replacement by a new civic religion, the Cult of Reason.[88] This Revolutionary co-opting of the sacred is evident throughout the play, nowhere more clearly, perhaps, than in the Roman sans-culotte's profession of faith: "Le Dieu des sans-culottes, c'est la liberté, c'est l'égalité, c'est la fraternité" (The God of the sans-culottes is freedom; it is equality; it is fraternity!).[89] The sans-culottes reject the existence of God or any other form of transcendence but not without elevating in their place new objects of worship: liberty, equality, fraternity—quintessential Enlightenment and republican values. Likewise, the principles of the French Revolution are described in the play as sacred ("sacrés") and the words written on the rock by the old man as saintly ("saints").[90] Religion still binds (in accordance with its etymology) but to enlightened civic values rather than transcendental rulers. The old man's sun cult fits this agenda. In the words of Perovic, "instead of fearing the volcano as an instrument of punishment, the old man teaches the savages to worship a more enlightened religion based on the sun. The sun, like the volcano, consists of fire but it is also light, that is a fire that burns without burning."[91] If the volcano, as an instrument of punishment and destruction of the pope and kings, is reminiscent of the dechristianization campaign, then the sun cult stands for its complement, the Cult of Reason, a secular religion without temples or priests (the savages swore never to have any, no more than kings) that yields enlightenment, not fear.[92] Indeed, while Maréchal and his play are often associated today with dechristianization, they were also closely linked to the Cult of Reason. Among other ties, Maréchal helped organize and spoke at the famed Festival of Reason held in Notre-Dame; he wrote a play entitled *La Fête de la raison* praising the new Cult; and *The Last*

Judgment of Kings was performed as part of another Festival of Reason in Rouen.[93]

Few symbols are as polysemic as the sun, however, and the solar cults that appear with astonishing frequency in Maréchal's writings do not always indicate a rejection of transcendence in favor of a secular civic religion. For instance, Maréchal begins his *Hymnes pour les 36 fêtes décadaires*, a work commissioned by Robespierre to choreograph the festivals of the new Cult of the Supreme Being that replaced the atheistic Cult of Reason, with the image shown in figure 1. The sun no longer symbolizes the light of human reason; instead, it manifests the existence of an eternal, transcendental power. Even after the fall of Robespierre, Maréchal continued to defend the Cult of the Supreme Being during which, he claimed, the "God of free men" had smiled upon the people through the disc of the sun.[94] The meaning of the solar cult in Maréchal's play is thus difficult to pin down, especially as there are hints throughout of a transcendental force at work. The very notions of a "prophecy" and a "last judgment" encourage the spectator to imagine a divine judge, a supreme entity who punishes the wicked and rewards the virtuous (hence, the old man expresses amazement at the providential order that exists on the island and has kept him safe from the savages, the beasts, and the volcano).[95] This is especially true given the last judgment in the play follows the biblical model, with the old man in the role of the prophet "who lived before the age of redemption and was saved in the Christian Last Judgment," and the wicked not just engulfed in lava but also cast into the bowels of the earth, that is, into the depths of hell.[96] Such an ending betrays Maréchal's vacillations: the play's volcano and its incarnation of an external, transcendental power could hardly be further from the original parable, in which the kings kill each other because they cannot live according to the immanent dictates of reason and equality.

Maréchal's play constitutes therefore the perfect introduction to the ever-changing but always complex relationship between

Figure 1. Frontispiece to Sylvain Maréchal's *Hymnes pour les
36 fêtes décadaires* (Paris: Basset, 1794).

the French Revolution and religion. Certain scenes display the
atheistic materialism of the dechristianization period. Others
brim with religion . . . or rather, religions plural, with some elements suggestive of the Cult of Reason and others of the Cult
of the Supreme Being. Such hybridity speaks to Maréchal's

struggle, and that of the Revolution as a whole, with how best to root out religious beliefs and practices so deeply engrained in the French people. Again and again in his writings, Maréchal seeks to find an elusive balance between his personal beliefs (atheism) and the perceived political wisdom of preserving, at least temporarily, some form of religion. The latter concern leads him to distance himself from the more virulent facets of the dechristianization campaign—including the derisive, carnivalesque spectacles that he had incorporated into his play—out of fear that they were fostering sympathy for martyred priests and deterring Christians, still the near totality of the French population, from fully embracing the Revolution. Treating priests with utter indifference, even forgetting them, would weaken the church more effectively than persecuting them. The same concern also explains his misgivings about the Cult of Reason, which he supports intellectually, even prophesying it will one day become universal, but which strikes him as a step too far and too fast for a people that still feels the need to believe in a divine power.[97] Setting aside his atheism, Maréchal intuits that dechristianization must not entail—not yet at least—complete secularization, that rather than destroy sacrality, the Revolution must transfer it to the right object, with his play identifying several new suitable gods: Reason, Liberty, Equality, Nature, Nation, or a Supreme Being at the source of it all. Maréchal's *Last Judgment of Kings* thus brings to the fore a vital phenomenon that the period's much-publicized attacks on the Catholic Church often obscure, what Mona Ozouf has called the Revolution's "transfer of sacrality": less an attempt to extinguish the people's sense of the sacred than to harness it into a new civic cult, through new forms, rituals, and stories that quite often closely imitate those of Catholicism.[98]

THE FESTIVE VOLCANO

Judging by newspaper reports on the play's reception, attending *The Last Judgment of Kings* was itself a ritual act that bound spectators through the experience of a common mythos and the collective outpouring of republican emotions. As Jomand-Baudry has noted, the play thus fulfilled the same functions as the famous festivals of the French Revolution. In fact, it borrowed many elements from these ceremonies, notably the volcano, which evoked the bonfires lit at the end of solemn, civic festivals to symbolically consume the attributes of the Ancien Régime, as well as the stakes where caricatural effigies were burned during more carnivalesque festivals.[99] This dual set of echoes illustrates one of the play's unique qualities: its mixing of elements from the two principal types of Revolutionary festivals, described by Marjorie Gaudemer as the "great" festival—official, respectable, bourgeois—and the "other" festival—derisive, violent, plebeian.[100] The first, the "civic" festival, is especially evident in the opening four scenes of the play, replete as they are with didactic speeches, common republican symbols and platitudes, and a genuine spirit of celebration and communion, as shown by the sans-culottes' tendency to speak "ensemble" and "à la fois" (together and at once), their identities melding into a single voice, a public opinion. The second, the "carnivalesque" festival, dominates the final four scenes, beginning with the arrival of the kings, and can be seen in the procession of shackled rulers, the ridiculously extravagant costumes, the sexual and physical humor, and the parodying of trials, duels, and executions.[101] Maréchal's play thus provides a fascinating window into perhaps the most significant cultural phenomenon of the French Revolution: festival culture.

Beyond borrowing widely from festival culture, as many other dramatic works did, *The Last Judgment of Kings* also played a largely forgotten role in a fascinating debate on the proper form and function of Revolutionary festivals. On January 20, 1794, there arose (rather belatedly) a discussion at the Jacobin Club about what, if anything, should be done the following day to commemorate the first anniversary of Louis XVI's death. The proposals, all performative in their own ways, ranged from the effortlessly symbolic (swearing an oath to "kill all tyrants," wearing red liberty caps, or gathering under a liberty tree to sing a patriotic anthem) to the more involved and representational (making effigies of the European kings at war with France and beheading them, as Louis XVI had been, or compelling all theaters to perform *The Last Judgment of Kings*). The latter two suggestions were rebuffed, although the Jacobins did send a delegation to the Commune to request that it "invite" the theaters in Paris to stage Maréchal's play.[102] The next day, on the actual anniversary of the king's execution, the entire Jacobin Club appeared before the National Convention to thank the Montagnards for their role in the capital sentence against Louis and to ask that a festival be celebrated annually on January 21. After swearing the same oath to "kill all tyrants," the deputies unanimously agreed to establish a new national festival and to accompany the Jacobins to sing patriotic anthems beneath the liberty tree at the Place de la Révolution, where the king had been executed.[103] This impromptu festival was interrupted however by the four executions scheduled that day, forcing the deputies to confront real repetitions of the legal violence they had come to commemorate. Some welcomed this touch of realism, but many reacted with disgust, lamenting that they had come to celebrate the death of a cannibal, not become one like him. The very idea of a commemoration, they now realized, was counterproductive at a time when the French needed to forget the king once and for all.[104] The Jacobins returned to their club, where they closed the historic day with two further decisions: first, that the liberty tree at the Place de la Révolution, which had been planted by Louis XVI, be uprooted and replaced by a new, untainted tree, and second, that four of their members be tasked with drawing up formal indictments against the remaining monarchs, the content of which would be sent to the tribunal of public opinion of every nation, in preparation for the kings' trial and punishment.[105]

It is worth delving deeper into this great variety of proposals and events, as they perfectly capture the diverse forms and functions attributed to the festivals of the Revolution. Many of the proposals betray an intense desire to repeat the event they seek to celebrate. The Jacobin who called for the creation and decapitation of effigies of European monarchs may have been ignored, but his wish was realized, as the first anniversary of the king's death was marked all over France through carnivalesque festivals that included "figures made of straw without heads, as reminders of the fate of Louis."[106] Demanding that *The Last Judgment of Kings* be performed as part of the festival stems from the same impulse: as we saw earlier, the play repeats the trial, judgment, and execution of the French monarchs. The dream of such festivals is to reenact the past—not just to commemorate it but truly resurrect it in the present. Hence the delight among some deputies that Louis's execution was celebrated not only through mimetic repetition (effigies and actors) but, even better, through real executions in the exact spot where he had perished, the Place de la Révolution. Hence too the Jacobin Club's plan to indict, try, and punish the remaining kings of Europe, which would bring Maréchal's play to reality and replicate Louis's fate. This longing for the constant reactivation of the past into the present is, according to Ozouf, typical of the parodic, carnivalesque festivals that dominated the fall and winter of 1793 before largely disappearing in the spring of 1794.[107] It inspired Marie-Joseph Chénier's speech on November 5, 1793, calling on the National Convention to establish yearly festivals retracing and reviving the history of the Revolution.[108] Fifteen days later, the *Feuille du salut public*, a mouthpiece for the government, urged theaters to emulate festivals by reenacting key Revolutionary events onstage.[109] Such ritual repetitions were meant to eternalize the Revolution by defining both the present and the future as an infinite reiteration of a fixed, recent past.

Other elements however do not repeat the king's death but suggest instead a symbolic displacement. What better example of this than the Jacobin Club's decision to cut down a tainted liberty tree rather than the head of the king (or his peers) who had planted it? The emphasis on abstract symbols—oaths, red caps, patriotic anthems—which are in no way connected to Louis's death but belong rather to the stock choreography of official civic festivals hints at a reluctance to confront the violence of the king's beheading. This is confirmed by the anger directed by most deputies at the real executions that disrupted their peaceful stroll to sing under a tree. It also explains why in subsequent years the National Convention established a strictly regulated, laconic, abstract festival, in which, according to Lynn Hunt, "there were no manikins, no parodies, no literal representations of violence."[110] To burn effigies of the king or to perform a play with a similarly fiery end for his peers, as some members of the Jacobin Club had proposed, struck the deputies as too evocative of the real, too literal a repetition of the bloody end that had befallen the king. Better to ignore these proposals and treat the spectators instead to didactic speeches and generic loyalty oaths, a purely symbolic festival that erased the violence at the heart of the event being commemorated.

Even the king was erased from his own festival: "The processions marched on, lost among the Brutuses, Liberties, Rousseaus, Franklins, and a few rare Monarchies. And were there any actual Louis XVIs? Even fewer."[111] A similar absence haunted the first performances of Maréchal's play. Surprisingly, for reasons that remain unclear, the two passages which referred most explicitly to the French monarchs—when the sans-culottes inform the old man that Louis has been guillotined, and when the old man recounts Marie-Antoinette's lack of empathy for his family's plight—were left out of the initial performances. If the king's erasure could still be explained by a reluctance to remember the violence perpetrated against him, the anecdote about Marie-Antoinette vindicated her execution without evoking its violence. Why then delete her from the play? Rather than what Graham E. Rodmell bizarrely calls "a moment of delicacy,"[112] the queen's erasure hints at another reason for the scarcity of French monarchs in the festivals and plays of the

Terror: not just an ambivalence toward violence but also an intense fear of resurrection. Dramatic or festive representations of sovereigns, aristocrats, and priests, however ridiculous and depraved they were made to seem, gave a second life to social categories that were no longer supposed to exist. To repeat the death of the king meant to revive him, even if only to execute him again. It went against the longing to eradicate and forget the Ancien Régime that had inspired, in the same period, the exhumation and obliteration of the cadavers of French kings and queens at the Basilica of Saint-Denis. (What better illustrates the Revolutionaries' fear of resurrection than this drive to destroy would-be royal zombies?) By foregrounding symbols and allegories and national heroes—a parade of Rousseaus and Liberties with nary a Louis to be seen—the Revolutionaries thus inverted the traditional function of festivals, from repeating and celebrating the past to burying it once and for all.[113]

Indeed, the king's absence from his own festival helped erase not only his violent end but also the ugly divisions that had surrounded it. Giving kings and queens a platform, even if that platform was a scaffold, only encouraged their supporters to regard the contentious trial and execution of Louis XVI as an ongoing debate rather than a clean break with the Ancien Régime. Like so many other pivotal moments of the Revolution, the king's trial had laid bare some profound disagreements not only between royalists and Revolutionaries but also between different factions of the latter, as former friends and allies splintered and turned upon one another. By focusing on generic, nondivisive allegories and symbols in lieu of a man who had inspired months of angry debate at the National Convention and many private tears after his death, the festivals sought to rewrite the history of the Revolution to give an impression of greater unity among its protagonists. To quote Béatrice Didier, "Les fêtes permettent la commémoration, une représentation au second degré, dans un temps qui n'est plus exactement celui de l'Histoire mais devient celui du mythe" (festivals enable commemoration, a representation in the second degree, in a time that is no longer exactly that of History but becomes that of myth).[114] *The Last Judgment of Kings*, especially the first half of the play, stages this kind of festival, offering a new founding myth for the Revolution: "[le peuple] a dit: *je ne veux plus de roi*; et le trône a disparu" (the people said, *We no longer want a king. And the throne disappeared*). In this myth, unlike in the History of the Revolution, the people speak as one; there is no conflict, no splintering into factions, no bloodshed, with the throne magically disappearing and the other monarchs obliterated by the volcano. One finds instead a ritualistic belief in the performative power of symbols and words ("the people said") also evident in the didactic speeches, oath swearing, and patriotic emblems in the play. Through its content—abstract, generic, "civic" festival in the first half; resurrective, parodic, "carnivalesque" festival in the second—*The Last Judgment of Kings* makes visible the tension in the Revolutionary era between two distinct, near-opposite conceptions of the festival and its function. Interestingly, the progression in the play from a civic to a carnivalesque festival (and indeed, the play is remembered almost exclusively today for its carnivalesque scenes) goes counter to the actual evolution in festival culture. Fall 1793, when the play was performed, marked the heyday of carnivalesque festivals, but as we saw in the debates on the celebration of Louis's death, the government increasingly rejected festivals of the sort in favor of more abstract, civic ones. *The Last Judgment of Kings* played a role in these debates, owing to its popularity and content, thereby echoing and influencing a pivotal moment in the history of Revolutionary festivals.

AN ERUPTION OF LAUGHTER, OR THE VOLCANO'S LAST LAUGH

The volcano is, by far, the most memorable addition to Maréchal's initial parable, and it transforms not only the story's plot but its overall impact as well. In the parable, the monarchs resign themselves to manual labor as the sole means of survival on the island but soon fall back into their bad habits, waging war upon one another until (this is the final line) "le genre humain, spectateur tranquille, eut la satisfaction de se voir délivré de ses tyrans par leurs propres mains" (the human race, a calm witness, had the satisfaction of seeing itself freed from these tyrants by their own hands).[115] The spectator's tranquility underscores the fact that the parable, as befits the genre, is not intended to arouse laughter or terror but rather quiet contemplation at the moral lesson that it contains. The kings' self-destruction may be instructive and satisfying, but nothing about it is comic. By contrast, in the play, the volcano offers a fitting end to a series of scenes that seek to elicit hilarity through comedic strategies (inversion, profanation, the grotesque body, animalization, etc.) that belong to the "culture of popular laughter" famously identified by Mikhail Bakhtin in his analyses of the carnival and the masterpieces of François Rabelais and Pieter Bruegel the Elder. The volcano, by sending kings in chains tumbling down a stage trap, reminds Gaudemer of fairground spectacles, where popular audiences could see wild animals paraded on a leash and returned to their cages through similar traps.[116] The parallel seems apt, given how many contemporaries of Maréchal also likened the procession of kings in the play to the parading of bears at the fair. Other scholars, as we saw earlier, associate the volcano with traditional elements of the carnival, from the flame-throwing balloons representing hell to the stakes lit on fire to consume caricatural effigies.[117] Even more obvious is the debt that the royal brawls in the play owe to the popular comedic genres of the farce and the Guignol. What had been serious and moralistic in the parable— the violence of despotism turning inward to destroy those who lived by it—evolves onstage into a slapstick scuffle leading not to destruction but derision. Fairground spectacle, carnival, farce, Guignol, satire—all belong to the same culture of popular laughter so central to *The Last Judgment of Kings*.

Or, it would be more accurate to say, central to the second half of *The Last Judgment of Kings*, for indeed, the comic ending diverges not only from the initial parable but also from the first four scenes of Maréchal's play, which contain no attempt at humor of any kind. Once again, the play can be split into two parts, illustrating two major strands of Revolutionary drama and two broad attitudes toward laughter. Scenes I to IV belong to the "theater of republican virtue," variously labeled as "ideological," "moralizing," "didactic," "utopian," "enlightened," and "grandiloquent," among other terms used to describe the soaring sermons of civic devotion and patriotism that comprise its core.[118] This theater strives, through long inspiring speeches and edifying examples of Revolutionary heroism, to kindle a political communion in its audience. Laughter has no place in these exaltations of civic virtue, and indeed, while comedies remained hugely popular throughout the Revolution, they were viewed with deep suspicion by the authorities, for whom laughter still seemed aristocratic and reactionary. This view reflects the influence of the Enlightenment distrust of theatrical laughter, evident in the development of the "genre sérieux" and in the condemnation of comedy by the likes of Diderot, Rousseau, and Mercier.[119] This condemnation had four main prongs: laughter breeds inequality between those who are in on the joke and those who are the butt of it; it fosters conformity to social prejudices and superficial codes of conduct under threat of mockery; it inspires resentment in the ridiculed and arrogance in the ridiculer; and it relies on wordplay and deception at odds with the philosophes' ethics of sincerity and transparency.[120] For these reasons, it does not belong in a republican play, any more than it does in a republican society.

Once the kings arrive in scene V, and as the republican sans-culottes slowly fade away from center stage, comedy and action replace solemnity and speech.[121] Yet this comedy looks nothing like the refined wit, erudite allusions, and subtle repartee associated with the highest echelons of the French monarchy, drawing instead from its inverse: Bakhtin's culture of popular laughter. Indeed, it displays many of the elements identified by Bakhtin as integral to popular laughter, such as the animalization of the kings that we noted earlier (as dancing bears) and that continues throughout the play (including comparisons to parasitic hornets, twenty ferocious animals, conniving beasts, and creatures in a menagerie devouring each other). They are further animalized through the emphasis placed on their grotesque bodies, wholly dominated by primary needs and urges. In the words of the Sardinian sans-culotte, "Voilà à quoi ils sont bons, tous ces rois; boire, manger, dormir, quand ils ne peuvent faire du mal" (This is all they're good for, all these kings; drinking, eating, and sleeping, when they cannot do any harm).[122] The marmot king (Victor Amadeus III, ruler of Sardinia) sleeps onstage; the sovereign of Spain wolfs down a piece of rye bread; all the monarchs brawl over a barrel of crackers. To this list of basic bodily functions can be added sex, with Catherine II in particular constantly reduced to her libido. The costumes (prosthetic noses and stomachs that deform and dehumanize) and the acting (grimaces and other exaggerated gestures, like Catherine's giant strides) also encourage the spectators to regard the kings solely as bodies, as pure matter devoid of spirit and thus sacrality.[123]

Situating the common people on the side of the spirit (exalted oratory, abstract virtue, symbolism) and kings on the side of the body constitutes an inversion of the traditional order—another key characteristic of popular laughter, according to Bakhtin. Inversion is everywhere in the play, although nowhere as clearly, perhaps, as in the procession scene, in which the people, earlier described as "men[és] en laisse comme des chiens de chasse" (led on a leash like hunting dogs), now walk their former masters with chains around their necks.[124] In fact, in his letter in the *Révolutions de Paris*, Maréchal himself presents inversion as the inspiration for his play: "CITOYENS, rappelez-vous donc comment, au temps passé, sur tous les théâtres on avilissait, on dégradait, on ridiculisait indignement les classes les plus respectables du peuple-souverain, pour faire rire les rois et leurs valets de cour. J'ai pensé qu'il était bien temps de leur rendre la pareille, et de nous en amuser à notre tour. Assez de fois ces *messieurs* ont eu les rieurs de leur côté" (Citizens, remember how, in times past, the most respectable classes of the sovereign people were debased, degraded, and disgracefully ridiculed on every stage to make kings and their court lackeys laugh. I thought it about time to return the favor, and for it to be our turn to amuse ourselves. On too many occasions have these *gentlemen* had the laughter on their side).[125] This prefatory quote reveals that inversion governs not only the play's interior (its content) but its exterior as well: the kings and courtiers who formerly watched and laughed at the people now find themselves onstage, being watched and laughed at by the same people who have taken their seats in the audience. The mere act of transposing real sovereigns from the halls of power to a theatrical stage constituted a degrading inversion in the eighteenth century, but it was made all the more humiliating by casting them in a farce, the lowliest—and most popular—literary genre.[126]

Maréchal's letter also positions his play as a response to aristocratic laughter and its former monopoly on French theater in the form of classical comedy. The socially divisive and unequal laughter of the court belongs to "times past," making the rise of a new theater necessary. Interestingly, the split nature of *The Last Judgment of Kings* testifies to the period's uncertainty about what this Revolutionary theater might look like. One option, illustrated by the first half of the play, entails a complete evacuation of laughter in the name of a theater of republican virtue. Another, exemplified by the second half, seeks to reclaim laughter and convert it into a weapon against the aristocracy by tapping into an older, formerly devalued culture of popular laughter. Such was the aim of the dozens of comedies modeled on Maréchal's play (or at least its second half) that proved impactful and trendy enough in the fall and winter of 1793 to be seen as an independent subgenre, labeled "pièces de dérision" or "théâtre de dérision carnavalesque" (derisive plays or theater of carnivalesque derision).[127]

Today, Maréchal's play is almost exclusively remembered for its application of comedic strategies from popular culture to subject matters and individuals associated with high culture—a co-opting of laughter rather than its elimination. Yet even that embrace of laughter is far more tentative and ambiguous than might first appear. After centuries of *The Last Judgment of Kings* being unfairly depicted as the height of vulgarity,[128] most scholars today underline instead the remarkable absence in the play of verbal excesses or obscenities, with the sans-culottes in particular speaking the language of the National Convention, not that of the streets.[129] What vulgarity exists in the play originates with the kings themselves, who insult and battle each other in farcical ways. The sovereigns are thus the source as well as the target of the derision, leaving the old man and the sans-culottes in the role of tranquil spectators, untainted by laughter. The sans-culottes do not (for the most part) mock the captive kings because such derision, however effective as a weapon, would too closely resemble the cruel, exclusory, and above all unequal laughter of the aristocracy. Their tributes to lofty ideals like generosity, transparency, and equality throughout the first half of the play make it unthinkable for them to assume the role of aristocrats (much like the old man had earlier refused to become king). This reluctance to switch positions highlights the way in which the play ultimately departs from the Bakhtinian carnival to which it is so often compared. In the carnival, the inversion of king and people, of mocker and mocked, is temporary and serves to release stresses in the social system, which it thus protects. Laughter maintains the unequal structure of the Ancien Régime even when it inverses, momentarily, the position of the participants in that structure. By contrast, in *The Last Judgment of Kings*, laughter, like the kings that employ and embody it, is self-destroying. Once the kings have permanently vanished, having ridiculed one another to the point of violence instead of sharing the crackers and toiling cooperatively on the island, true equality can begin, without the divisions and differences on which laughter depends. The volcano thus constitutes a last laugh, a final eruption of laughter in a comedy that seeks— or, to use its title, that prophesizes—the end of comedy.

THE VOLCANO BURNS OUT: ON THE END(S) OF PROPAGANDA

If the volcano is remembered for anything today, it is above all as a perfect illustration of a now pervasive practice that first appeared, according to most historians, during the French Revolution: political propaganda.[130] What makes the volcano such a fitting emblem of the period's propaganda? First, the volcano served as a visible incarnation of the towering might of a political faction, the Mountain. This geological analogy was not new— in a famous speech at the National Convention, Pierre Gaspard Chaumette had exhorted the Mountain to "become a volcano"— but more than any document, speech, or artwork, Maréchal's play helped popularize it.[131] Second, the volcano was only able to spew its fire onstage thanks to the government's direct involvement in the arts. As we noted earlier, the Committee of Public Safety requisitioned twenty pounds each of saltpeter and gunpowder and ordered their delivery to the Théâtre de la République, suggesting that it placed more importance in the play's "propagation des principes républicains" (propagation of republican principles) than in the desperate pleas by soldiers on the front lines for functioning firearms.[132] In lieu of saltpeter and gunpowder, some of these soldiers likely received one of the 6,000 copies of Maréchal's play purchased and sent to the troops by the War Ministry, in the hope that such a shipment would ignite, if not their guns, then at least their spirits. In so doing, the War Ministry followed the example of the Committee of Public Safety, which had already sponsored 3,000 copies of the play, much as it funded throughout the second half of 1793 numerous engravings and pamphlets ridiculing the European monarchs who had joined forces against the French republic.[133] Legend has it, in fact, that the government became so involved that it sent three deputies of the National Convention to the Théâtre de la République to force a recalcitrant actor, Grandmesnil, to perform in the play, under threat of death by hanging. There is no evidence corroborating this story beyond the claims of a single vulgarized history of the French Revolution published fifty years after the fact, but however apocryphal the tale may be, its very acceptance and repetition by many scholars show the degree to which Maréchal's play has become synonymous with propaganda.[134]

Indeed, with very few exceptions,[135] researchers have depicted *The Last Judgment of Kings*, and Revolutionary drama more broadly, as "a propaganda machine."[136] If the aim of such a theater truly was to move and mold public opinion into perfect, passionate alignment with the views and decisions of the government, then judging by some reviews, Maréchal's play fully realized its ambitions: "le parterre et la salle entière paraissaient composés d'une légion de tyrannicides, prêts à s'élancer sur l'espèce *léonine*, connue sous le nom de rois" (the parterre and the entire audience seemed composed of a legion of tyrannicides, poised to throw themselves upon the leonine species known as kings).[137] But then a question arises: Why, if playing to packed, ecstatic audiences with the active support of the government, did the play suddenly disappear from Parisian stages after February 20, 1794? If the "propaganda machine" was operating exactly as intended, why turn it off after only twenty-one performances?[138] Many tentative explanations have been put forward. Jacques Truchet hypothesizes that the powder and saltpeter proved too scarce for the government to dispense with, although he also repeats a claim by Paul d'Estrée, made without any supporting evidence, that the Committee of Public Safety banned the play to avoid causing displeasure to foreign governments that now seemed open to negotiating with the

French republic.[139] Or perhaps the play vanished from Parisian stages because of its treatment of domestic kings, not foreign ones. As we saw earlier, January 1794 marked a turning point in the Revolutionaries' conception of commemoration, which increasingly came to be seen as an instrument of symbolic displacement and erasure rather than as a means of repetition or even remembrance. Little surprise, then, that a repetition of regicide as violently transparent as the one in Maréchal's play would come to an end less than a month later.[140]

Other scholars have noted—quite sensibly given the volatility of Revolutionary politics—that a play could be perfectly aligned with the government in October 1793 and out of favor just a few months later. This was especially true for a play so closely associated with the sans-culottes and the dechristianization campaign, two positions with far greater official support in mid-October 1793, when the play premiered, than in the weeks that followed. The speed and extent of the transformation in the government's stance on religion must have stunned Maréchal: as early as November, Robespierre and other Montagnards began denouncing the excesses of the dechristianization campaign and accusing atheists of secretly serving the counterrevolutionary cause of aristocrats and foreign powers.[141] By December 1793, the Committee of Public Safety was actively forbidding anti-religious plays, including Maréchal's *La Fête de la raison*, which was banned just moments before the start of its premiere on December 31, 1793, more for the whiff of atheism in its title than for anything especially offensive in its content.[142] In this context, it is surprising that a play praised by Jacques Hébert and other dechristianizers for its anticlericalism even survived until February 1794, although it perhaps only did so because there had been no new performances since December 19, 1793, so that one might argue that the play had disappeared long before its last hurrah on February 20.

Yet there exists another possible explanation for the play's disappearance: not just that it no longer echoed the views of the government but also that it no longer accorded with how the government wished to convey these views. Indeed, *The Last Judgment of Kings* became embroiled in a debate on the nature and extent of state involvement in the arts. The authorities' shifting reactions to the play encapsulate a wide range of relationships to the theater and provide thereby a microcosmic history of government-theater interaction during the Revolution. In a review of *The Last Judgment of Kings*, the *Feuille du salut public* offers perhaps the best insight into the government's understanding of propaganda in fall 1793: "L'esprit public existe enfin, mais il ne peut se soutenir qu'en tournant les esprits *uniquement* vers la révolution, qu'en se pénétrant de ce principe sévère, que celui-là est *justiciable du tribunal révolutionnaire qui veut distraire de la chose publique*" (A public spirit exists at last, but it can only be sustained by turning minds *solely* toward the Revolution, by interiorizing the strict principle that whoever *seeks to distract from public affairs is prosecutable by the Revolutionary Tribunal*).[143] In this view, the value of art lies exclusively in the politics of its content and the content of its politics. Through a mix of threats (prosecution) and rewards (such as saltpeter, gunpowder, and printing subsidies), the government seeks to ensure that plays speak solely of the Revolution and only to praise it. This particular form of instrumentalization of the arts had already been enshrined into law on August 2, 1793, with a decree stipulating that all theaters would henceforth perform at least three patriotic plays per week (especially plays "qui retracent les glorieux événements de la Révolution" [that retrace the glorious events of the Revolution]), while any that staged plays with royalist or anti-revolutionary leanings would be shut down and their directors imprisoned.[144] The summer and fall of 1793 thus saw the rise of the kind of governmental involvement in the arts that we associate today with propaganda: the patronage, even sometimes the imposition, of specific themes and topics, with the aim of shaping the political views of the citizenry, to such a degree, in fact, that plays lacking a clear political message were rejected as suspicious distractions.

An early sign of a shift in cultural policy can be glimpsed in the proposal on November 24, 1793, by the president of the National Convention, Gilbert Romme, that the Committee of Public Instruction be tasked with examining which plays were most conducive "à former l'esprit et les mœurs du peuple" (to forming the minds and morals of the people).[145] Romme's proposal was promptly shot down on the grounds that it would introduce a form of censorship that was not only illegal but also unnecessary when one could simply trust in the people's judgment, the soundness of which needed no further proof than the success of *The Last Judgment of Kings*. In November 1793, Maréchal's play thus remained for many at the National Convention the single best example of good republican theater. Yet the emphasis in Romme's proposal on morality rather than just politics heralded a different conception of state involvement, one that would hold a far less favorable view of *The Last Judgment of Kings* and of derisive theater in general. Indeed, starting in late December 1793, the Committee of Public Safety set out on a campaign to purge the French stage of vulgar, immoral plays that hid their pernicious attacks on the people's virtue behind impeccably republican politics. On January 15, 1794, the Committee decreed that "les théâtres doivent être l'école de la vertu et des mœurs; les directeurs et les acteurs sont responsables des abus qui se commettent sur la scène" (theaters must be schools of virtue and morals; directors and actors are accountable for any excesses committed onstage). Over the weeks that followed, it summoned directors and actors to demand that they transform their theaters into "une école de mœurs et de décence" (a school of morals and decency), even arresting a few for having staged improper plays.[146] The "school of virtue" metaphor long predates the Revolution, of course, but its prevalence in January and February 1794 signals a shift from a purely political surveillance to a more moralistic and aesthetic involvement that must have felt at once less and more intrusive. On the one hand, it only defined what ought not be done and punished transgressors after the performance, a lighter touch than mandating what had to be done (i.e., perform certain plays or topics). On the other hand, it broadened the scope of the government's involvement from the content of plays, their political declarations, to *how* that content was delivered and received, the quality and propriety of the acting and staging and their supposed impact on the spectators' virtue. This should not be seen as a movement away from the political, however, but rather as a sign that, by 1794, everything, including morality and aesthetics, had become political. A few months later, the Committee of Public Instruction would issue a broad and forceful condemnation of "l'hébertisme des arts," by which it meant the bad taste and loose morals—epitomized by the lowbrow, physical humor and the obscenities in derisive plays like *The Last Judgment of Kings*—that had been encouraged or at least tolerated in the name of a political instrumentalization of the dramatic arts.

The Last Judgment of Kings thus supports Mark Darlow's assertion that "we can no longer speak of the arts of the Revolutionary decade as pure state propaganda."[147] If "pure" propaganda is defined as the direct imposition of political dogma by and for organs of the state in an effort to shape public opinion, then no play would seem to better illustrate this model than the (at first) state-sponsored *Last Judgment of Kings*. For the same play to have fallen victim shortly thereafter to a different kind of governmental meddling reveals that the Revolutionary state did not follow a coherent cultural policy but vacillated instead between rival conceptions of the role of the arts in society (from political mouthpiece to school of virtue to site of aesthetic distraction). The label of pure propaganda seems in any case quite ill fitting for a play whose heteroglossia I hope to have made evident in this introduction. While *The Last Judgment of Kings* transports key figures, events, and debates of the Revolution to the stage, it refrains from offering a single clear answer or interpretation. Indeed, it is precisely the qualities that make it impure or unpredictable as propaganda—above all, its tendency to raise questions rather than foreclose them—that also make it the perfect window into the multifaceted, protean world of the French Revolution.

NOTES

1. In a recent article, Pawel Matyaszewski observes that out of the eight hundred plays created between 1789 and 1794, *The Last Judgment of Kings* serves to this day as an almost obligatory "exemple idéal" (ideal example), "texte modèle" (model text), and "texte de référence par excellence" (a reference text par excellence). Pawel Matyaszewski, "La possibilité d'une île, ou le *Jugement dernier des rois* de Sylvain Maréchal (1793)," *Cahiers ERTA* 22 (2020): 72.

2. Two editions of the play were published in 1793—the first (the one we transcribed) by the printer C.-F. Patris in Paris and the second by the printer J. Labbé in Vienna. The two texts are identical and were the only ones published during Maréchal's lifetime. Louis Moland included the play in his 1877 *Théâtre de la Révolution* but without any critical apparatus beyond two short paragraphs in a broad introduction to Revolutionary theater. Louis Moland, *Théâtre de la Révolution* (Paris: Garnier frères, 1877). Daniel Hamiche reproduced the play, with a dozen footnotes, as an appendix to his monograph *Le Théâtre et la Révolution*. Daniel Hamiche, *Le Théâtre et la Révolution: La lutte de classes au théâtre en 1789 et 1793* (Paris: Union Générale d'Editions, 1973). The only proper edition of *The Last Judgment of Kings* can be found in a collection of eighteenth-century plays that Jacques Truchet published in the Bibliothèque de la Pléiade in 1974. Jacques Truchet, *Théâtre du XVIIIe siècle*, vol. 2, coll. Bibliothèque de la Pléiade (Paris: Gallimard, 1974). However, this two-volume collection spans over three thousand pages and is out of print and usually out of stock (save for rare copies on secondhand sites sold at prohibitive prices). None of these editions features an English translation.

3. Sanja Perovic asserts that *The Last Judgment of Kings* "is cited in most books on the Revolution." Sanja Perovic, *The Calendar in Revolutionary France: Perceptions of Time in Literature, Culture, Politics* (Cambridge: Cambridge University Press, 2012), 17. Graham E. Rodmell describes the play as "more written about than read." Graham E.

Rodmell, *French Drama of the Revolutionary Years* (London: Routledge, 1990), 35. Likewise, Jean-Marie Apostolidès notes that Maréchal's oeuvre is "souvent mentionnée, peu lue et rarement interprétée" (often mentioned, little read and rarely performed). Jean-Marie Apostolidès, "La guillotine littéraire," *French Review* 63, no. 4 (1989): 985. Indeed, I know of only one modern performance of the play: a staging by students of the French department at King's College London, under the direction of Sanja Perovic, as the finale of a conference on June 5, 2015, entitled "The French Revolution Effect."

4. Hamiche was the first to make this claim, which has since often been repeated as fact. Hamiche, *Le Théâtre et la Révolution*, 176. However, Emmet Kennedy calls the claim that *The Last Judgment of Kings* was viewed by no fewer than 100,000 spectators an "hyperbolic error of judgment." Emmet Kennedy, Marie-Laurence Netter, James P. McGregor, and Mark V. Olsen, *Theatre, Opera, and Audiences in Revolutionary Paris: Analysis and Repertory* (Westport, CT: Greenwood Press, 1996), 6.

5. Philippe Bourdin, *Aux Origines du théâtre patriotique* (Paris: CNRS, 2017), 462; Jean-Marie Apostolidès, "Theater and Terror: *Le jugement dernier des rois*," in *Terror and Consensus: Vicissitudes of French Thought*, ed. Jean-Joseph Goux and Philip R. Wood (Stanford, CA: Stanford University Press, 1998), 137; Rodmell, *French Drama*, 165; Hamiche, *Le Théâtre et la Révolution*, 174–176.

6. Endlessly repeated, including by some who never bothered to read the actual decree by the Committee of Public Safety, the story evolved to imply that the saltpeter and gunpowder were gifted by the government. In reality, the decree states that the directors of the Théâtre de la République would have to repay the value of such precious commodities. Cited in Guillaume Cot, "La Scène et la Loi: les dramaturgies du droit (1789–1794)" (PhD diss., Université Paris VIII, 2021), 598.

7. Henry Lumière, *Le Théâtre français pendant la Révolution* (Paris: Dentu, 1894), 220.

8. For a sampling of these virulent criticisms, see those cited in Truchet, *Théâtre du XVIIIe siècle*, 1557; Marjorie Gaudemer, "La dramaturgie propagandiste, étude de cinq pièces militantes de la Terreur" (master's thesis, Université Paris X, 2001–2002), 24; and Stéphanie Fournier, *Rire au théâtre à Paris à la fin du XVIIIe siècle*, coll. L'Europe des Lumières (Paris: Classiques Garnier, 2016), 574–576.

9. Matyaszewski, "La possibilité d'une île," 72.

10. Maurice Dommanget, *Sylvain Maréchal: L'égalitaire, "L'homme sans Dieu," sa vie, son oeuvre (1750–1803)* (Paris: Cahiers de Spartacus, 1950), 258.

11. Serge Bianchi, "Le Théâtre de l'an II (culture et société sous la Révolution)," *Annales historiques de la Révolution française* 278 (1989): 432.

12. Hamiche, *Le Théâtre et la Révolution*, 184; Bianchi, "Théâtre de l'an II," 432.

13. Paul Eugène Jauffret, *Le Théatre Révolutionnaire (1788–1799)* (Paris: Furne, Jouvet, 1869), v.

14. Cot, "La Scène et la Loi," 555.

15. Sylvain Maréchal, *Almanach des Honnêtes Gens* (Paris, 1788).

16. Hence, according to Perovic, "Maréchal's first published works were imitations—of Gessner's *Bergeries*, of Montesquieu's *Le Temple de Gnide*, and of a popular sixteenth-century text, *Le livre de tous les âges ou le Pibrac moderne*." Sanja Perovic, "Sylvain Maréchal (1750–1803)," The Super-Enlightenment: A Digital Archive, accessed April 22, 2023, https://exhibits.stanford.edu/super-e/feature/sylvain -marechal-1750-1803.

17. In fact, on the night of its premiere, *The Last Judgment of Kings* was performed before *Le Méchant* (it was customary in the eighteenth century for two plays—the first shorter than the second—to be performed the same evening).

18. Jacques Proust, "Le jugement dernier des rois," in *Approches des Lumières* (Paris: Klincksieck, 1974), 377–378.

19. Dommanget, *Sylvain Maréchal*, 266.

20. Matyaszewski, "La possibilité d'une île," 82–83.

21. Charles Collé, *La Partie de chasse de Henri IV* (Paris: Didot, 1778).

22. Claude-Marie-Louis-Emmanuel Carbon de Flins Des Oliviers, *Le Réveil d'Épiménide à Paris* (Toulouse: Broulhiet, 1790). On this genre of plays, see Susan McCready, "Performing Time in the Revolutionary Theater," *Dalhousie French Studies* 55 (2001).

23. Louis-Sébastien Mercier, *L'An 2440, rêve s'il en fut jamais* (Londres, 1771).

24. See pp. 85, 119.

25. Jean-Jacques Rousseau, *Du Contrat social*, ed. Bruno Bernardi (Paris: GF Flammarion, 2001), 46.

26. Montesquieu, *Lettres persanes*, ed. Laurent Versini (Paris: GF Flammarion, 1995), 53–62.

27. *Feuille du salut public*, October 20, 1793; *Révolutions de Paris*, August 3–October 28, 1793; *Affiches, annonces, et avis divers*, October 19, 1793; Louis-Sébastien Mercier, *Le Nouveau Paris*, vol. 3 (Brunswick: Chez les principaux libraires, 1800), 220.

28. See pp. 92, 126.

29. On the trope of the Revolutionary cannibal, see Cătălin Avramescu, *An Intellectual History of Cannibalism* (Princeton, NJ: Princeton University Press, 2009); Eli Sagan, *Citizens and Cannibals: The French Revolution, the Struggle for Modernity, and the Origins of Ideological Terror* (New York: Rowman & Littlefield Publishers, 2001); and Antoine de Baecque, *La Gloire et l'effroi* (Paris: Grasset, 1977), 77.

30. For a longer list of imitators, see Dommanget, *Sylvain Maréchal*, 269–271.

31. Matyaszewski, "La possibilité d'une île," 73; Martin Nadeau, "La politique culturelle de l'an II: les infortunes de la propagande révolutionnaire au théâtre," *Annales historiques de la Révolution française* 327 (January–March 2002): 64; Suzanne J. Bérard, "Aspects du théâtre à Paris sous la Terreur," *Revue d'Histoire littéraire de la France* 4/5 (1990): 615; Beatrice F. Hyslop, "The Theater during a Crisis: The Parisian Theater during the Reign of Terror," *The Journal of Modern History* 17, no. 4 (1945): 346; Anne Coudreuse, "Insultes et théâtre de la Terreur: l'exemple du *Jugement dernier des rois* (1793) de Pierre-Sylvain Maréchal," in *Les insultes: bilan et perspectives, théorie et actions*, ed. Dominique Lagorgette (Chambéry, France: Presses universitaires Savoie Mont Blanc, 2016), 30; McCready, "Performing Time," 27; Rodmell, *French Drama*, 34; Dommanget, *Sylvain Maréchal*, 260; Truchet, *Théâtre du XVIIIe siècle*, 1557; Jacques Proust, "De Sylvain Maréchal à Maiakovski: contribution à l'étude du théâtre révolutionnaire," in *Studies in Eighteenth-Century French Literature* (Exeter, UK: University of Exeter, 1975), 215; Apostolidès, "La guillotine littéraire," 985; Mark Darlow, "Staging the Revolution: The Fait historique," in "Revolutionary Culture: Continuity and Change," ed. Mark Darlow, special issue, *Nottingham French Studies* 45, no. 1 (Spring 2006): 80; Guy Bruit, "89–93: Quel Théâtre?," *Raison Présente* 91 (1989): 101.

32. Jauffret, *Théâtre Révolutionnaire*, 257; Moland, *Théâtre de la Révolution*, xxiii, 299; Gaudemer, "La dramaturgie propagandiste," 22; Pierre Frantz, "Rire et théâtre carnavalesque pendant la Révolution," *Dix-Huitième Siècle* 32 (2000): 303; Sylvain Maréchal, *Anti-Saints: The New Golden Legend of Sylvain Maréchal*, trans. with an introduction

by Sheila Delany (Edmonton: University of Alberta Press, 2012), 9; Hamiche, *Le Théâtre et la Révolution*, 171, 191; Béatrice Didier, "Sylvain Maréchal et le *Jugement dernier des rois*," in *Saint-Denis ou le Jugement dernier des rois*, ed. Roger Bourderon (Saint-Denis, France: Editions PSD Saint-Denis, 1993), 131; Perovic, *The Calendar in Revolutionary France*, 127; Fournier, *Rire au théâtre*, 574; Catherine Ailloud-Nicolas, "Scènes de théâtre: *Le Tremblement de terre de Lisbonne* (1755), *Le Jugement dernier des rois* (1793)," in *L'invention de la catastrophe au XVIIIe siècle: Du châtiment divin au désastre naturel*, ed. Anne-Marie Mercier-Faivre and Christiane Thomas (Genève: Droz, 2008), 412; Françoise Aubert, *Sylvain Maréchal: Passion et Faillite d'un Égalitaire* (Pise-Paris: Goliardica-Nizet, 1975), 22; Michèle Sajous D'Oria, "Les bouffons des rois," in *La Participation dramatique: Spectacle et espace théâtral (1730–1830)*, coll. L'Europe des Lumières (Paris: Classiques Garnier, 2020), 237.

33. Régine Jomand-Baudry states October 17 on page 235 but writes just a few pages later that the play was performed two days after the queen's execution. Régine Jomand-Baudry, "Désacralisation et transfert du sacré dans *Le Jugement dernier des rois* de Sylvain Maréchal," in *Le Sacré en question: Bible et mythes sur les scènes du xviiie siècle*, ed. Béatrice Ferrier (Paris: Classiques Garnier, 2015), 235–251; likewise, in *Theatre, Opera, and Audiences*, Kennedy first states October 18 on page 43 and then October 17 on page 197.

34. Hamiche and Didier wrongly argue that scholars who disagree with them must have failed to understand that ads appearing in newspapers on the seventeenth were in fact for a performance the following day. Hamiche, *Le Théâtre et la Révolution*, 191; Didier, "Sylvain Maréchal," 130.

35. See the *Journal des Spectacles*, October 19, 1793; the *Journal de Paris*, October 20, 1793; the *Moniteur universel*, October 30, 1793; and the *Abréviateur universel*, October 31, 1793. The repertories CÉSAR (*Calendrier électronique des spectacles sous l'Ancien Régime*) and André Tissier, *Les Spectacles à Paris pendant la Révolution* (Geneva: Droz, 2002), 75, also identify October 17 as the day of the premiere.

36. See pp. 76, 110.

37. "L'exemple des Français a fructifié" (The French example has borne fruit). See pp. 80, 114.

38. Fournier, *Rire au théâtre*, 579.

39. Scholars who have made this claim include Jomand-Baudry, "Désacralisation et transfert," 5; Apostolidès, "Theater and Terror,"

138; Perovic, *The Calendar in Revolutionary France*, 127; and Mary Ashburn Miller, *A Natural History of Revolution: Violence and Nature in the French Revolutionary Imagination, 1789–1794* (Ithaca, NY: Cornell University Press, 2011), 158.

40. Sylvain Maréchal, *Correctif à la Révolution* (Paris: Chez les Directeurs de l'Imprimerie du Cercle Social, 1793), 112. For a political interpretation of this passage, see Cot, "La Scène et la Loi," 572.

41. Yann Robert, *Dramatic Justice: Trial by Theater in the Age of the French Revolution* (Philadelphia: University of Pennsylvania Press, 2019).

42. Fournier, *Rire au théâtre*, 579; Pascal Dibie, "Le peuple fait le spectacle: Le théâtre révolutionnaire de Pierre Sylvain Maréchal (1750–1803)," in *Le peuple existe-t-il?*, ed. Michel Wieviorka (Auxerre, France: Éditions Sciences Humaines, 2012), 83–99.

43. Thomas Paine, for instance, wishes to see the king exiled to the United States, while Louis-Sébastien Mercier prefers Tahiti.

44. "Leur supplice eût été trop doux et aurait fini trop tôt" (Their torture would have been too gentle and too quick). See pp. 82, 116.

45. "Vous auriez dû, sur des échafauds, mourir tous de mille morts: mais où se serait-il trouvé des bourreaux qui eussent consenti à souiller leurs mains dans votre sang vil et corrompu?" (You should have all died a thousand deaths on the scaffold, but where could we have found executioners who would have agreed to soil their hands with your vile and corrupted blood?). See pp. 91, 125.

46. "Il a paru plus convenable d'offrir à l'Europe le spectacle de ses tyrans détenus dans une ménagerie et se dévorant les uns les autres, ne pouvant plus assouvir leur rage sur les braves sans-culottes qu'ils osaient appeler leurs sujets. Il est bon de leur donner le loisir de se reprocher réciproquement leurs forfaits, et de se punir de leurs propres mains" (It seemed more suitable to offer Europe the spectacle of its tyrants held in a menagerie, devouring each other, no longer able to relieve their anger on the brave sans-culottes they had dared to call their subjects. It is good to give them the leisure to blame each other for their own crimes and to punish each other by their own hands). See pp. 82, 116.

47. "Cette cinquantaine de personnages ne vécut pas longtemps en paix; et le genre humain, spectateur tranquille, eut la satisfaction de se voir délivré de ses tyrans par leurs propres mains" (This group of fifty-odd characters did not live in peace for long; and the human

race, a calm witness, had the satisfaction of seeing itself freed from these tyrants by their own hands). See pp. 68, 102.

48. Thomas Paine, *Opinion de Thomas Payne sur l'affaire de Louis Capet* (Paris: Imprimerie nationale, 1793), 6.

49. On the narrative of social rehabilitation in early Revolutionary drama, see Robert, *Dramatic Justice*, 331.

50. See pp. 82, 116.

51. Proust, "De Sylvain Maréchal à Maiakovski," 218.

52. Apostolidès, "La guillotine littéraire," 990–992. Miller, *A Natural History of Revolution*, 157–159. See also David McCallam, *Volcanoes in Eighteenth-Century Europe: An Essay in Environmental Humanities*, Oxford University Studies in the Enlightenment (Liverpool: Liverpool University Press, 2019), 177.

53. Miller, *A Natural History of Revolution*, 159. "The Mountain" refers to the left-leaning radical group at the National Convention. I use the term *Montagnards* elsewhere to describe its members. Strangely, Miller argues that the volcano destroys not only the monarchs but also the innocent savages—a sign that the Revolutionaries perceived and feared the indiscriminateness of naturalized violence. In fact, the review of the play in the *Journal des spectacles* of October 19 makes clear that the savages, who reside on a different island, are not harmed by the volcano: "les sauvages quittent aussi la place, les rois demeurent seuls" (the savages also leave the place; the kings remain alone). There does not seem to be, therefore, any tension or ambiguity in Maréchal's embrace of the volcano as a metaphor for the violent justice of the Terror.

54. *Feuille du salut public*, October 20, 1793.

55. Didier, "Sylvain Maréchal," 136.

56. Erica Joy Mannucci, "Revolution and the Last Judgement," in *The Languages of Revolution*, ed. L. Valtz Mannucci (Milan: Università degli studi di Milano, 1989), 243.

57. See in particular *Abréviateur universel*, October 31, 1793, and *Journal des spectacles*, October 22, 1793.

58. The volcano "realises the myth that it is ultimately nature's decree and not the vote of the Convention which put Louis XVI to death." McCallam, *Volcanoes*, 169. See also Perovic, *The Calendar in Revolutionary France*, 127, 143; and Frantz, "Rire et théâtre," 303.

59. Frantz, "Rire et théâtre," 303.

60. This is the term used by Fournier. Fournier, *Rire au théâtre*, 588.

61. Cot, "La Scène et la Loi," 601.

62. Perovic, *The Calendar in Revolutionary France*, 78; McCallam, *Volcanoes*, 159; Miller, *A Natural History of Revolution*, 140, 148.

63. Sylvain Maréchal, *Les Antiquités d'Herculanum avec leurs explications en françois* (Paris: Chez David, 1780).

64. "All the elements that would characterize the subsequent republican calendar were already in place [in Maréchal's 1788 *Almanach des Honnêtes Gens*]: the ten-day week, the 'numerical' months, the secular festivals, and the belief that rupture would release a new source of time that would regenerate all of mankind." Perovic, *The Calendar in Revolutionary France*, 42.

65. Cot, "La Scène et la Loi," 584.

66. Apostolidès, "Theater and Terror," 139.

67. Perovic, "Sylvain Maréchal (1750–1803)."

68. See pp. 80, 113. For an analysis of this passage, see Darlow, "Staging the Revolution," 82; McCallam, *Volcanoes*, 168; and Perovic, *The Calendar in Revolutionary France*, 143.

69. This conception of revolution as a singular moment of rupture appears in many of Maréchal's works, and nowhere more clearly perhaps than in these verses from his *Hymnes pour les 36 fêtes décadaires*: "L'ainé de toute la famille / A dit: je ne veux plus de Rois / Ni de verrous ni de Bastille: / Aussitôt dit, aussitôt fait, / Le voilà libre pour jamais" (The firstborn of the family / Said: I no longer want any kings / Nor locks nor Bastille: / No sooner said than done, / Here he is forever free). Sylvain Maréchal, *Hymnes pour les 36 fêtes décadaires* (Paris: Basset, 1794), 6.

70. *The Last Judgment of Kings* was the first play to designate itself a "prophétie," and one of only two in the entire Revolution. Gaudemer, "La dramaturgie propagandiste," 47.

71. The play transports its spectators to "l'époque heureuse et prochaine de la chute et du châtiment des rois" (the happy and imminent era of the fall and punishment of kings). *Feuille du salut public*, October 20, 1793. It is "une prophétie que le génie de la liberté, aidé du courage des républicains français, ne doit pas tarder à vérifier" (a prophecy that liberty's genius, assisted by the courage of French republicans, will not take long to verify). *Affiches, annonces et avis divers*, October 19, 1793. After all, Maréchal is already famous for "des prophéties qui ont eu leur entier accomplissement" (prophecies that were entirely realized), and under the right circumstances, "la fiction théâtrale ne tarderait pas à devenir un fait historique" (the theatrical fiction would soon become historical fact). *Révolutions de Paris*, August 3–October 28, 1793.

72. See pp. 73, 107. Apostolidès, "La guillotine littéraire," 987; Cot, "La Scène et la Loi," 592; Gaudemer, "La dramaturgie propagandiste," 51.

73. See pp. 84, 118.

74. Didier, "Sylvain Maréchal," 134.

75. Maréchal, *Correctif à la Révolution*, 8. See also Maréchal's *Dame nature*, where the same categories are described as the two "extremes" of humanity. Sylvain Maréchal, *Dame Nature à la barre de l'Assemblée Nationale* (Paris: Chez les marchands de nouveauté, 1791), 10.

76. Maréchal, *Dame nature*, 4; Maréchal, *Correctif à la Révolution*, 12.

77. Aubert, *Sylvain Maréchal*, 95.

78. Maréchal, *Correctif à la Révolution*, 6.

79. Maréchal, *Correctif à la Révolution*, 49.

80. McCready, "Performing Time," 28.

81. Proust, "De Sylvain Maréchal à Maiakovski," 219.

82. Perovic comes to a similar conclusion when she writes that Maréchal understands rupture "as a periodic regeneration of time, as a new creation that would abolish history and return society to the mythic time of a golden age." Perovic, *The Calendar in Revolutionary France*, 85.

83. McCallam, *Volcanoes*, 171.

84. Didier, "Sylvain Maréchal," 131–132.

85. McCallam, *Volcanoes*, 179.

86. The violation of the royal tombs in Saint-Denis took place from October 14 to 25, 1793, with the Bourbon crypt opened on October 16, the day before the premiere of *The Last Judgment of Kings*. The order to remove all religious symbols, statues, and crosses was decreed on October 14, 1793, just two days earlier. McCallam, *Volcanoes*, 167; Rodmell, *French Drama*, 170.

87. Fournier, *Rire au théâtre*, 587.

88. On interpretations of the Cult of Reason, see Perovic, *The Calendar in Revolutionary France*, 156.

89. See pp. 91, 125.

90. See pp. 80, 114; 77, 111.

91. Perovic, *The Calendar in Revolutionary France*, 143.

92. Matyaszewski notes the symbolism of the transition from a religious ritual performed at dusk to one that elevates the savages to the top of a white rock and literally drags them out of the darkness and into the light. Matyaszewski, "La possibilité d'une île," 84–85.

93. Delany, introduction to *Anti-Saints*, 9; Hamiche, *Le Théâtre et la Révolution*, 175.

94. Dommanget, *Sylvain Maréchal*, 286.

95. See pp. 75, 109.

96. Mannucci, "Revolution and the Last Judgement," 242.

97. Dommanget, *Sylvain Maréchal*, 275–287.

98. On Maréchal's play as an illustration of Ozouf's "transfer of sacrality," see Jomand-Baudry, "Désacralisation et transfert."

99. Jomand-Baudry, "Désacralisation et transfert," 2, 10; Fournier, *Rire au théâtre*, 586; Gaudemer, "La dramaturgie propagandiste," 53.

100. Gaudemer, "La dramaturgie propagandiste," 63–64.

101. Gaudemer, "La dramaturgie propagandiste," 48–50.

102. The invitation appears to have fallen on deaf ears, as there were no performances of the play in January 1794. Lynn Hunt studies the debate at the Jacobin Club on how to commemorate the king's death but she does not mention the proposal that Maréchal's play be performed. Lynn Hunt, *The Family Romance of the French Revolution* (Berkeley: University of California Press, 1992), 62. Only one article mentions this proposal, and this solely in passing. Sajous D'Oria, "Les bouffons des rois," 242.

103. These events are described in *Messager du soir*, January 21, 1794; *Feuille du salut public*, January 22, 1794; *Journal des hommes libres de tous les pays*, January 22, 1794; and *Moniteur universel*, January 23, 1794.

104. Hunt, *Family Romance*, 62–64.

105. *Messager du soir*, January 22, 1794.

106. Hunt, *Family Romance*, 63.

107. Mona Ozouf, *Festivals and the French Revolution*, trans. Alan Sheridan (Cambridge, MA: Harvard University Press, 1988), 92.

108. Bruit, "89–93: Quel théâtre?," 104.

109. *Feuille du salut public*, November 20, 1793.

110. Hunt, *Family Romance*, 64.

111. Ozouf, *Festivals and the French Revolution*, 175.

112. Rodmell, *French Drama*, 220.

113. On the fear that Revolutionary plays, by reenacting current events, were resurrecting vanquished foes and breathing new life into settled conflicts, see Robert, *Dramatic Justice*, 360–361.

114. Didier, "Sylvain Maréchal," 129.

115. See pp. 68, 102.

116. Gaudemer, "La dramaturgie propagandiste," 59.

117. See the earlier section on the festive volcano. According to Sajous
D'Oria, the carnival constitutes the principal "clé de lecture"
(reading key) for *The Last Judgment of Kings*. Sajous D'Oria, "Les
bouffons des rois," 252.

118. Gaudemer, "La dramaturgie propagandiste," 48, 55; Fournier, *Rire
au théâtre*, 582.

119. Frantz, "Rire et théâtre," 291.

120. Robert, *Dramatic Justice*, 51–54; Antoine de Baecque, *Les Éclats du
rire: La culture des rieurs au XVIIIe siècle* (Paris: Calmann-Lévy,
2000); Jean Goldzink, *Comique et comédie au siècle des Lumières*
(Paris: L'Harmattan, 2000).

121. Fournier, *Rire au théâtre*, 583–584; Coudreuse, "Insultes et théâtre,"
35–36; Gaudemer, "La dramaturgie propagandiste," 48.

122. See pp. 88, 122.

123. *Abréviateur universel*, October 31, 1793.

124. See pp. 80, 114.

125. See pp. 69, 103.

126. On the play as an illustration of Bakhtin's carnival, see, among
others, Frantz, "Rire et théâtre," 295; Gaudemer, "La dramaturgie
propagandiste," 55–57; and Proust, "Le jugement dernier des rois," 376.

127. Bérard, "Aspects du théâtre," 615; Frantz, "Rire et théâtre," 293;
Gaudemer, "La dramaturgie propagandiste," 112; Annette Graczyk,
"Le théâtre de la Révolution française, média de masses entre 1789 et
1794," *Dix-huitième Siècle* 21 (1989): 404.

128. In 1931, Félix Gaiffe condemned Maréchal's play as "les dernières
limites de la grossièreté dans le comique" (the ultimate extremes of
coarseness in comedy), cited in Rodmell, *French Drama*, 158.

129. Sajous D'Oria, "Les bouffons des rois," 252; Truchet, *Théâtre du XVIIIe
siècle*, 1559; Didier, "Sylvain Maréchal," 134–135; Bruit, "89–93: Quel
théâtre?," 102; Coudreuse, "Insultes et théâtre," 32; Frantz, "Rire et
théâtre," 303.

130. Gaudemer, "La dramaturgie propagandiste," 7.

131. Miller, *A Natural History of Revolution*, 149; Apostolidès, "La
guillotine littéraire," 990; McCallam, *Volcanoes*, 173; Sajous D'Oria,
"Les bouffons des rois," 241.

132. François Aulard, ed., *Recueil des Actes du Comité de Salut Public*, vol. 8
(Paris: Imprimerie nationale, 1895), 413.

133. Sajous D'Oria, "Les bouffons des rois," 250.

134. The story first appears in Augustin Challamel and Wilhelm Tenint,
Les Français sous la Révolution (Paris: Challamel Editeur, 1843), 271.

It is repeated by Victor Hallays-Dabot, *Histoire de la censure théâtrale en France* (Paris: E. Dentu, 1862), 184; Paul d'Estrée, *Le Théâtre sous la Terreur* (Paris: Émile-Paul frères, 1913), 12; Hamiche, *Le Théâtre et la Révolution*, 220; Fournier, *Rire au théâtre*, 579; and Sajous D'Oria, "Les bouffons des rois," 238.

135. Darlow cites a couple in a footnote. Darlow, "Staging the Revolution," 77.

136. McCready, "Performing Time," 26. See also Graczyk, "Le théâtre de la Révolution française," 401; and Rodmell, *French Drama*, 33, 206. Gaudemer cites six other scholars who used the term propaganda to designate Revolutionary theater. Gaudemer, "La dramaturgie propagandiste," 15.

137. *Feuille du salut public*, October 20, 1793.

138. We noted earlier the confusion about the exact date of the play's premiere. By contrast, there is broad agreement on the number of performances that followed: a total of twenty-one representations during the play's first run, with the last performance on February 20, 1794. The play's second and final run was even more short-lived: a single performance in January 1796. CÉSAR; Tissier, *Spectacles*, 75; Kennedy, *Theatre, Opera, and Audiences*, 197.

139. Truchet, *Théâtre du XVIIIe siècle*, 1559; Estrée, *Le Théâtre sous la Terreur*, 247; Gaudemer, "La dramaturgie propagandiste," 63; Fournier, *Rire au théâtre*, 589–590.

140. This is Darlow's theory. Darlow, "Staging the Revolution," 81.

141. Bianchi, "Théâtre de l'an II," 430.

142. Graczyk, "Le théâtre de la Révolution française," 404–405; Frantz, "Rire et théâtre," 302; Bérard, "Aspects du théâtre," 617–618; Dommanget, *Sylvain Maréchal*, 283.

143. *Feuille du salut public*, October 20, 1793.

144. Graczyk, "Le théâtre de la Révolution française," 397; Bérard, "Aspects du théâtre," 611–612; Nadeau, "Politique culturelle," 62; Gaudemer, "La dramaturgie propagandiste," 14–15.

145. *Messager du soir*, November 24, 1793.

146. Fournier, *Rire au théâtre*, 569–570; Bérard, "Aspects du théâtre," 617–618; Frantz, "Rire et théâtre," 300–301; *Moniteur universel*, February 4, 1794.

147. Darlow, "Staging the Revolution," 77.

The Last Judgment

of Kings

A prophecy in one act, in prose,

BY P. SYLVAIN MARÉCHAL,

PERFORMED at the Théâtre de la République, during the month of Vendémiaire and the days that followed.

———

TANDEM! . . .

———

IN PARIS,

From the printing house of C.-F. PATRIS, PRINTER of the Com. rue du Faubourg St.-Jacques, at the ci-devant Dames Ste.-Marie.

———

YEAR 2 of the FRENCH REPUBLIC, one and indivisible.

NOTICE
To the theater directors of the departments.

————

The author, undersigned, reserves the rights afforded to him by a decree of the National Convention on performances of his play by the different theaters of the republic.

Sylvain Maréchal

Nota. The passages in the play indicated by quotation marks are not recited at the Theater.

THE CONCEPT of this play is taken from the
following Parable in *LESSONS FOR THE ELDEST CHILD
OF A KING*, a philosophical work by the
same author, published at the beginning of 1789,
and placed on the INDEX by the Police.[1]

———

In those days: having returned from the court very tired, a madman[2] fell asleep and dreamt that on the Day of Saturnalia all the peoples of the Earth came to an agreement to independently seize their kings. At the same time, they convened a general meeting to gather this handful of crowned individuals and relegate them to a small, uninhabited—but habitable—island, whose fertile soil only needed manpower and simple farming. A cordon of small armed boats was established to keep an eye on the island and prevent the new settlers from leaving. The difficulties of the newly landed monarchs were not slight. They started by stripping themselves of all their royal adornments that encumbered them; and to survive, each one had to put his

1. It bears noting that this parable was written and published before the French Revolution. Although Maréchal refers here to the second edition of his book, published in Brussels in 1789, the first edition dates back to 1788 and already contains the same parable, entitled "A Vision. The Deserted Island."

2. The original French "visionnaire" has been translated in accordance with its meaning in the eighteenth century, when it referred to a person with false visions and extravagant ideas rather than, as it does today, to someone with a premonition of the future. *Dictionnaire de l'Académie française*, 1762.

shoulder to the wheel. No more valets, no more courtiers, no more soldiers. They had to do everything themselves. This group of fifty-odd characters did not live in peace for long; and the human race, a calm witness, had the satisfaction of seeing itself freed from these tyrants by their own hands,—*pages 30–31.*

THE AUTHOR
OF
*THE LAST JUDGMENT
OF KINGS,*
TO the spectators of the first performance of this play.

———

CITIZENS, remember how, in times past, the most respectable classes of the sovereign people were debased, degraded, and disgracefully ridiculed on every stage to make kings and their court lackeys laugh. I thought it about time to return the favor, and for it to be our turn to amuse ourselves. On too many occasions have these *gentlemen* had the laughter on their side; I thought it was now time to make them the laughingstock of the public, and in so doing to parody a just verse from the comedy *Le Méchant*:

Kings are here on earth for our entertainment.

GRESSET[3]

This is the reason for the slightly *exaggerated* parts of THE LAST JUDGMENT OF KINGS.

(Excerpt from the newspaper *Les Révolutions de Paris*, by Prud'homme, volume 17, page 109, in-8°.)

———

3. The original verse parodied here, from Jean-Baptiste-Louis Gresset's *Le Méchant*, reads "Les sots sont ici-bas pour nos menus plaisirs" (Fools are here on earth for our entertainment; act 2, scene 1). Such was the popularity of Gresset's play that eighteenth-century audiences would have recognized the reference and the deliberate equation of kings with fools.

CHARACTERS' COSTUMES

THE EMPRESS: Gold silk moiré corset, puffed sleeves; blue taffeta skirt with the waistline decorated with *points d'Espagne* or gold lace; poppy-red satin or taffeta cloak with embellishments on the cuff as well as the skirt; neckline covered in linen, which forms the ruff; a military medal fastened at the waist of the coat; crown made of golden paillon; blue taffeta headpiece.

THE POPE: Bright red or white wool cassock and headpiece; linen rochet with lace; white gloves; white shoes with a golden double cross in the middle; poppy-red satin papal tiara with crowns of gold; a zucchetto of the same satin, covering the ears, with white fur trim; stole and maniple.

THE KING OF SPAIN: Spanish-style clothing, coat, breeches, leggings, and sandals, all in red; a large false nose in flesh-colored taffeta; gold silk moiré crown embellished with precious stones; three ribbons around the neck: the first, poppy red, with the insignia of the Golden Fleece; the second, sky blue with a medal; the third, black velvet with a medal.

THE EMPEROR: Blue clothing trimmed with gold; a ribbon around the neck with the insignia of the Empire; another white ribbon trimmed with two red lines worn over the shoulder; a poppy-red scarf resting on his shoulders; silk moiré crown; petticoat, breeches, and white stockings.

THE KING OF POLAND: Frock with black velvet sleeves; short puff-sleeved jacket in the same black velvet as the frock: on the jacket there must be an armor of white fur; knitted breeches made of crimson silk; ribbon of the order, black velvet, embellished with gold; a second ribbon worn over the shoulder, sky blue and of any order.

THE KING OF PRUSSIA: Dark blue clothing, buttoned up to the waist; a large tricorn hat; black plumet and cockade; gold *point d'Espagne* trim on his hat; yellow breeches; riding boots; hair styled in a tight ponytail; white satin scarf with golden fringe.

THE KING OF ENGLAND: Dark blue clothing with gold or brass buttons; likewise for the coat; stomach stuffed to make him appear fatter; riding boots; garter of the order *Honni soit qui mal y pense*; a military medal of the same order.

THE KING OF NAPLES: Spanish waistcoat; linen short-sleeved shirt; breeches in the same style as the waistcoat; Spanish jacket, poppy-red ribbon with a medal around the neck and a second ribbon around the neck in black velvet, embroidered in gold.

THE KING OF SARDINIA: Dressed as a financier; ribbon of the order around the neck; a military medal attached to the outfit; crowned with an ermine frontlet.

ONE SAVAGE (speaking part):[4] Silk-knit pants and cardigan, clearly striped; laced sandals; gray beard and gray wig.

EIGHT SAVAGES (characters without lines): With quivers and arrows.

4. Hamiche claims that the text should read "The old man" rather than "One savage" (Hamiche, *Le Théâtre et la Révolution*, 306). It is true that the costume described seems more fitting for the old man than for one savage (and why just one savage and not the others?), and that it is odd that the old man does not appear among the characters listed. Moreover, none of the savages has a "speaking part" in the play, unlike, of course, the old man. That said, why specify that the old man has a speaking part and not do so for any of the other characters (notably the sans-culottes and the kings)? Does this designation not suggest an attempt to distinguish one savage from the others who are described immediately after as "characters without lines"? The mystery remains unsolved.

TEN SANS-CULOTTES, each dressed in the style of the country whose king they are leading chained by the neck, that is, one Spanish sans-culotte, one German, one Italian, one Neapolitan, one Polish, one Prussian, one Russian, one Sardinian, one English, and one French.

A great number of the People, armed with sabers, rifles, and pikes, all dressed in the style of the French sans-culottes.

A barrel full of crackers.

CHARACTERS

AN OLD FRENCHMAN. . . . . *Monvel.*

SAVAGES of all ages and sexes.

A SANS-CULOTTE from each nation of Europe.

THE KINGS OF EUROPE, including

THE POPE. . . . . *Dugazon.*

THE CZARINA. . . . . *Michot.*[5]

THE EMPEROR. . . . .*Raymont.*

THE KING OF ENGLAND.

THE KING OF PRUSSIA.

THE KING OF NAPLES.

THE KING OF SPAIN. *Baptiste le jeune.*

THE KING OF SARDINIA.

THE KING OF POLAND. . . . .*Grand-Mesnil.*

5. To cast even more ridicule on poor Catherine II, her role was performed by a man, the popular comedian Antoine Michaut, alias Michot.

THE LAST JUDGMENT OF KINGS, PROPHECY IN ONE ACT

The scene represents the interior of an island half-destroyed by a volcano. At the back of the stage is a mountain from which fly sparks of fire every once in a while, from the start of the play to its end.

On one side, downstage, a few trees shade a hut, its rear wall sheltered by a big white rock, on which can be read this inscription, drawn with coal:

> Better to have for a neighbor
> A volcano than a king.
> Freedom. . . . Equality.

There are several numbers under the inscription. A stream cascades and flows alongside the cottage.

On the other side, a view of the sea.

The sun rises behind the white rock during the monologue of the OLD MAN, *who adds a number to those he has already drawn.*

FIRST SCENE

THE OLD MAN: *(He is counting.)* 1, 2, 3 . . . 19, 20. Today marks exactly 20 years since I was marooned on this deserted island. The despot who signed my order of banishment is perhaps dead by now . . . [6] Back in my poor

6. What despot is this? The question is more complex than it seems. Subtract twenty years from the date of the play's premiere, and the banishment of the old man occurred in fall 1773, under the reign of Louis

country, people think I have been burned to death by the volcano, torn to pieces by the teeth of some wild animals, or eaten by cannibals. To this day, however, the volcano, the predatory beasts, and the savages seem to have respected the victim of a king . . .

My good friends are slow to come, even though the sun has risen! . . . What's this I see? . . . These aren't their usual canoes . . . It's a lifeboat! . . . It's approaching, propelled by oars! White people . . . Europeans! . . . What if they were my people, French people . . . perhaps they are coming to look for me . . . The tyrant is perhaps dead; and as is commonly practiced at each new coronation, his successor, to make himself more popular, pardoned some of the innocent victims of the previous reign . . . I refuse the clemency of a despot: I would rather stay and die on this volcanic island than go back to Europe, at least so long as there remain kings and priests.

I will hide behind this rock! I must know why these people are here.

XV. Yet Truchet rejects this hypothesis, deeming it absurd that Maréchal would have wanted to target Marie Leszczynska, not Marie-Antoinette, in the passages where the old man excoriates the queen. Let us not forget, he cautions, that the play is a prophecy: "l'action se joue dans le futur, après la victoire totale de la République sur les rois; or il suffisait d'attendre le mois de mai 1794 pour que le souverain régnant vingt ans plus tôt devînt Louis XVI, et la reine Marie-Antoinette" (the action takes place in the future, after the total victory of the Republic over the kings, and in fact, one only needed to wait until the month of May 1794 for the king ruling twenty years prior to be Louis XVI and the queen, Marie-Antoinette). Truchet, *Théâtre du XVIIIe siècle*, 1561–1562.

SCENE II

Twelve or fifteen SANS-CULOTTES,[7] one from each European
nation. *(They disembark.)*

———

THE FRENCH SANS-CULOTTE: Let's see if this island will
do, the third that we have visited. It appears to have been
volcanic, and to be active still. All the better! The world
will be rid even sooner of all the crowned bandits whose
deportation has been entrusted to us.

THE ENGLISHMAN: It seems to me that this will suit them just
fine. Nature, by her own hands, will soon ratify and
sanction the sans-culottes' judgment against the kings,
these criminals so long privileged and unpunished.

THE SPANIARD: May they suffer here all the torments of hell,
in which they did not believe, but in which they made us
believe through the priests, their accomplices, just to make
us blind.[8]

THE FRENCHMAN: Brothers! This island seems inhabited . . .
Do you see these footprints?

THE SARDINIAN: At the entrance of this cave are some
freshly harvested fruits.

THE FRENCHMAN: My friends! Come! Come here; read:

> *Better to have for a neighbor*
> *A volcano than a king.*

7. The sans-culottes, thus named because they did not wear silk knee
breeches like the nobility and bourgeoisie, were Revolutionaries
belonging to the common people. Advocating a direct democracy and a
more egalitarian society, they wielded considerable influence on political
life, particularly between 1792 and 1794, through their involvement in
patriotic clubs, the petitions they drafted in the Revolutionary sections of
Paris and presented before legislative assemblies, and the recourse to
popular violence (or to the threat of such violence).
8. The original French "embêter" has been translated in accordance with its
meaning in the eighteenth century: "to make stupid, blind." *Littré*, 1873.

SEVERAL SANS-CULOTTES, *at the same time*: Bravo! Bravo!

THE FRENCHMAN, *continuing to read*:

> Freedom. . . . Equality.

Some martyr of the Ancien Régime must live here. What a fortunate encounter!

THE ENGLISHMAN: Oh! We landed in the right place! The man groaning on this island isn't expecting to meet his liberators today.

THE FRENCHMAN: The poor wretch has no idea: he would have died unaware of his country's liberation.

THE GERMAN: And all of Europe's. He must not be far: let us look for him; let us go meet him.

THE FRENCHMAN: I can't wait to meet him! He's surely one of us; and, judging from the saintly words he traced upon this rock, he is worthy of the great Revolution, since he was able to foresee it from the ends of the earth.

SCENE III
The previous characters and the OLD MAN.

————

SEVERAL SANS-CULOTTES, *at the same time*: Kind elder! . . . venerable old man! . . . what are you doing here?

THE OLD MAN: Frenchmen! . . . Oh, happy day! . . . it has been so very long since I have seen Frenchmen. My friends! My children! What do you seek? . . . but before anything else, perhaps a shipwreck has tossed you on this shore; are you in need of food? I have nothing to offer you but these fruits, and the water from this spring. My hut is too small to hold you all at once. I wasn't expecting such large and good company.

THE FRENCHMAN: Good father, we don't need anything. All we want is to listen to you, to know your story; afterward, we will tell you our own.

THE OLD MAN: Simply put, here it is: I am French, born in Paris. I lived on a small estate bordering the park of Versailles. One day, the hunt passes my way; the deer is chased into my garden. The king and all his people enter my home.[9] My daughter, tall and beautiful, is noticed by all these *gentlemen* of the court. The next day, they take her from me . . . I run to the palace to claim my daughter; they ridicule me; they turn me down; they chase me away. I am not discouraged; with a tear in my eye, I throw myself at the king's feet. A word about me is whispered in his ear; he laughs in my face and orders that I be removed. My poor wife is no more successful than I; she dies of sorrow. I return to the palace. I recount my grief to everyone. Nobody wants to get mixed up in it. I ask to speak to the queen; I seize her by the dress as she is leaving her apartments. Ah! she says, this irksome man again. When will he finally be banned from my presence?[10] I go before the clergy; I raise my tone; I speak as a man, as a father. One of them, it was a prelate, says nothing, but he makes a gesture. Some men arrest me at the door of his audience hall; they cast me into a dungeon, where I remained until I was thrown into the bottom of a ship which left me on this island in its wake, exactly twenty years ago today. There you have it, my friends, my adventure.

9. The old man's story constitutes a deliberate rewriting and inversion of Charles Collé's wildly popular royalist play, *La Partie de chasse de Henri IV*. For more on this topic, see the section "A Parodic Imagination" in the introduction to this edition.

10. A note at the beginning of the edition informs the reader that passages "indicated by quotation marks are not recited at the Theater." The first passage to have been omitted onstage goes from "I ask to speak" to "my presence."

THE FRENCH SANS-CULOTTE: Now that it is your turn to listen, know that you've been well avenged! To tell you everything would take too long. Here is the crux of the matter: Kind elder, you have in front of you a representative of each of the now free and republican nations of Europe, for you must know that there are no longer any kings in Europe.

THE OLD MAN: Is it really true? Could it be? . . . You are toying with a poor old man.

THE FRENCH SANS-CULOTTE: True sans-culottes honor old age, and never mock it . . . as the servile courtiers of Versailles, Saint James, Madrid, and Vienna once did.

THE OLD MAN: What! There are no longer kings in Europe? . . .

A SANS-CULOTTE: You will see them all disembark here; they are following us in the hold of a small armed ship (it is their turn, as it once was yours). We arrived first to prepare their dwelling. You will see them all here, with one exception.

THE OLD MAN: And why this exception? Not a one has ever been worth more than the others.

THE SANS-CULOTTE: You're right . . . *except one*, because we guillotined him.

THE OLD MAN: *Guillotined*! . . . What does that mean?

THE SANS-CULOTTE: We'll explain that, and plenty more:[11] We cut off his head, in the name of the law.

THE OLD MAN: The French have finally become men!

---

11. Second unrecited passage, from "You're right" to "plenty more."

THE SANS-CULOTTE: Free men. In a word, France is a republic, in the strongest sense of the term. The people of France rose up. They said, *We no longer want a king.* And the throne disappeared. They then said, *We want a republic*, and here we all are, republicans.

THE OLD MAN: I never would have dared hope for such a revolution, but I understand it. I have always thought to myself that the people, just as powerful as the God preached to them, only have to will it . . . How happy I am to have lived long enough to learn of such an amazing event. Ah! my friends! my brothers, my children! I am transported with joy!

But thus far you've only spoken of France, and it seems, if I've understood correctly, that all of Europe has been freed from the contagion of kings?

THE GERMAN: The French example has borne fruit, though it was not without difficulty. All of Europe came together against the French, not the peoples themselves, but the monsters who insolently claimed to be their *sovereigns.* These monsters armed all their slaves. They put into action every possible means to dissolve the kernel of freedom that Paris had formed. From the start, they slandered this generous nation that was the first to bring its king to justice. They wanted to tame it, federalize it, starve it, subjugate it once more, so that mankind would be forever disgusted at the thought of independent rule. However, after reflecting on the sacred principles of the French Revolution, after reading the sublime expressions and the heroic virtues that the Revolution engendered, the peoples of the other nations told themselves, "We've been such fools to let ourselves be driven to the slaughterhouse like sheep, or led on a leash like hunting dogs sent to fight a bull. Let us instead join forces with our elders in reason and in liberty." As a result, each part of Europe sent brave sans-culottes to Paris to represent it. There, in this assembly of all the peoples, it was agreed that on a certain day, all of Europe would rise up en masse and liberate itself . . . Indeed, a simultaneous general insurrection broke out in all the nations of Europe, and they each had their own 14th of July and 5th of October 1789, their own 10th of August and 21st of September 1792, their own May 31st and June 2nd of 1793.[12] We'll teach you about this era, the most astounding of all of history.

THE OLD MAN: What marvels! . . . For now, just satisfy my impatient curiosity on one point: I keep hearing you use the term "sans-culotte." What does this peculiar and striking expression signify?

THE FRENCH SANS-CULOTTE: That is for me to explain: A sans-culotte is a free man, the ultimate patriot. The masses, the true people, always good, always strong, are made up of sans-culottes. They are pure citizens, living on the edge of need, who earn their bread by the sweat of their brow, who love work, who are good sons, good fathers, good husbands, good relatives, good friends, good neighbors, but who are as adamant about their rights as they are about their duties. Until now, for lack of working together, they were just blind, passive instruments in the hands of the wicked: the kings, the nobles, the priests, the egotists, the aristocrats, the statesmen, the federalists, all people whose precepts and abominable crimes we'll tell you about,

---

12. The German sans-culotte lists here many of the most significant events of the French Revolution: the storming of the Bastille (14th of July 1789), the Women's March on Versailles (5th and 6th of October 1789), the storming of the Tuileries, the suspension of the king, and the creation of the National Convention (10th of August 1792), the abolition of the monarchy and the proclamation of the First Republic by this same Convention (21st of September 1792), and the insurrection that led to the Girondins' loss of power to the Montagnards, the Convention's new masters (31st of May and 2nd of June 1793).

wise and mistreated old man. Now in charge of tending to the hive, the sans-culottes no longer wish to suffer among them the cowardly, harmful, arrogant parasitic hornets.[13]

THE OLD MAN, *with enthusiasm*: My brothers, my children, then I too am a sans-culotte!

THE ENGLISHMAN, *continuing his tale*: The same day, therefore, each people declared itself a republic and established a free government. But at the same time, they proposed the organization of a European convention to be held in Paris, principal city of Europe. The first act proclaimed by the convention was the last judgment of the kings already detained in the prisons of their respective palaces. They were condemned to exile on a deserted island where they'll be guarded by a small fleet, each country taking a turn keeping watch over them while circling around the island, until the last one of these monsters is dead.[14]

THE OLD MAN: But tell me, I beg you, why did you bother to bring all these kings here? It would have been more expedient to hang them all, at the same hour, under the portico of their palaces.

THE FRENCH SANS-CULOTTE: No, no! Their torture would have been too gentle and too quick: it would not have fulfilled the goal that we had set. It seemed more suitable to offer Europe the spectacle of its tyrants held in a menagerie, devouring each other, no longer able to relieve their anger on the brave sans-culottes they had dared to call their *subjects*. It is good to give them the leisure to blame each other for their own crimes and to punish each other by their own hands. Such is the solemn and final judgment

13. Likely an echo of a metaphor employed by Jacques Hébert in his newspaper *Le Père Duchesne*. *Le Père Duchesne*, number 14, 1790.
14. This entire speech, from "The same day" to "is dead," was not performed.

that has unanimously been pronounced against them, and that we have come across these seas to execute.

THE OLD MAN: I give in; I am convinced.

A SANS-CULOTTE: Now that you are more or less up to date, tell us, kind elder, if this island that you have been inhabiting for twenty years would seem to you a suitable site to discharge our haul of worthless merchandise?

THE OLD MAN: My friends, this island is uninhabited. When I was cast ashore here, it was morning; I would not encounter any living being for the rest of the day. That evening, a canoe anchored at this small harbor. From it came several families of savages, of whom I was afraid at first. I hadn't done them justice; they soon dispelled my fears with a warm welcome. They promised to bring me every evening some of their fruit, game, or fish—for they came to this island every day at dusk to worship the volcano you can see over there. Without challenging their faith, I invited them to at least split their homage between the volcano and the sun. They did not fail to return early in the morning three days later to witness the phenomenon I had described to them, and to which they had never paid attention in their smoke-filled huts. I brought them to this white rock and made them contemplate the sun rising from the sea in all its glory. This sight filled them with ecstasy. Since that moment, not a week has passed without them coming to worship the rising sun.[15] Since then, too, they have regarded and treated me as their father, their doctor, their counsel—and thanks to them, I have lacked for nothing in this uncultivated solitude. Once, they fervently wanted to honor me as their king—I explained to them as

---

15. Several sentences, from "without challenging their faith" to "the rising sun," were left unsaid during the play's performances.

best I could my adventures, and they swore to me never to have any kings, nor any priests.[16]

I believe that this island will perfectly fulfill your intentions; especially since, for the past few weeks, the crater of the volcano has been steadily expanding and threatens, it would seem, to erupt imminently. Better for it to explode on crowned heads than on those of my good neighbors, the savages, or of my brothers, the brave sans-culottes.

A SANS-CULOTTE: Comrades, what do you say? I think he's right: let us signal the fleet so that it may meet us here and vomit the poison it is carrying.

THE OLD MAN: I can see my good neighbors. Lower your pikes before them as a sign of fraternity; you will see them drop their bows at your feet. I do not know their language and they are ignorant of ours, but the heart is of all countries; we communicate through gestures and understand each other perfectly.

Families of SAVAGES *come out of their canoes. The* OLD MAN *introduces them to the European* SANS-CULOTTES. *They fraternize; they embrace: the* OLD MAN *climbs up on his white rock and pays tribute to the sun for the fruits that the* SAVAGES *have brought him in skillfully woven wicker baskets.*

After the ceremony, the OLD MAN *converses with them through gestures and informs them of the plan.*

The KINGS *arrive: they appear onstage one by one, scepters in hand, royal cloaks on their shoulders, golden crowns on their heads, and, around each of their necks, a long iron chain that a* SANS-CULOTTE *holds by the end.*

---

16. This is likely an echo of Montesquieu's famous parable of the Troglodytes, which ends with a virtuous old man refusing to be crowned king. *Lettres persanes*, letter 14.

SCENE IV
The previous characters, families of SAVAGES.

———

THE OLD MAN: Brave sans-culottes, these savages are our elders in liberty as they have never had a king. Born free, they live and die as they were born.[17]

SCENE V
The previous characters, the KINGS of Europe.

———

A GERMAN SANS-CULOTTE, *leading the* EMPEROR *who opens the procession*: Make way for his majesty the emperor[18] . . . He only lacked some time, and a little more genius, to bring to completion all the crimes committed by the House of Austria, and to compound the evils that Joseph II[19] and Antoinette wished and unleashed upon France. He was the scourge of his neighbors just as he was of his own country, whose population and finances he bled dry. He wasted away its agriculture, shackled its economy, and enchained its spirit. *(Tugging on the* EMPEROR'S *chain.)* Unable to get the lion's share out of the partition of Poland, he decided to make up for it by ravaging the borders of another nation, whose energy and enlightenment he feared. A false friend and a treacherous ally, doing evil for doing evil's sake. He's a monster.

17. This description echoes a well-known sentence from Jean-Jacques Rousseau's *Social Contract*: "L'homme est né libre, et partout il est dans les fers" (Man is born free, and everywhere he is in chains).
18. Francis II (1768–1835): the Holy Roman emperor from 1792 to 1806 and a nephew of Marie-Antoinette, Francis II spent the first twenty-two years of his reign at war with France, losing in the process a large share of his titles and possessions.
19. Joseph II (1741–1790): the Holy Roman emperor from 1765 to 1790, he was the brother of Marie-Antoinette and the uncle of Francis II. An Enlightenment-inspired reformer, he does not appear in Maréchal's play, having died before 1793.

FRANÇOIS II: Excuse me? I'm not as much of a monster as people believe me to be. It's true that Lorraine tempted me, but wouldn't France have been happy enough to buy peace and order at the cost of a province? Doesn't she already have enough? At any rate, if there's someone to blame, it's that old Kaunitz who took advantage of my youth and of my inexperience: it's Cobourg; it's Brunswick.[20]

THE GERMAN, *releasing him*: You mean it's your villainous soul, your rotten heart . . . From now on you will live here, forever separated from humanity, upon whom you and your brothers have inflicted shame and suffering for too long.

AN ENGLISH SANS-CULOTTE, *leading the* KING OF ENGLAND *on a leash with a chain*: Behold his majesty the King of England,[21] who with the help of the Machiavellian genius of Mr. Pitt[22] drained the purse of the English people and increased the burden of the national debt so as to spark civil war, anarchy, famine, and, even worse, federalism in France.

GEORGE: But I had lost my head, you know that. Do we punish the insane now? No, we put them in an asylum.

THE ENGLISHMAN, *releasing him*: The volcano will restore you to reason.

---

20. Francis II here blames Wenzel Anton von Kaunitz (1711–1794), the state chancellor of the Habsburg monarchy; Prince Frederick Josias of Saxe-Coburg-Saalfeld (1737–1815), the field marshal of the Imperial Army; and Charles William Ferdinand, Duke of Brunswick (1735–1806), the field marshal of the combined armies of Prussia and Austria.
21. George III (1738–1820): the king of Great Britain from 1760 to his death in 1820, his rule was marked by numerous wars, most of them against France (the Seven Years' War and successive wars against Revolutionary and Napoleonic France). Even before the start of the Revolution, it was widely known that he suffered from a mental disorder.
22. William Pitt the Younger (1759–1806): the prime minister of Great Britain and a famed enemy of the French Revolution, he struck alliances against France and incited civil unrest there. In 1793, he was decreed an "enemy of the human race" by the National Convention.

A PRUSSIAN SANS-CULOTTE: Behold his majesty the King of Prussia.[23] Just like the Duke of Hanover,[24] he is a pernicious and conniving beast, the prey of all conmen and the executioner of all good and free men.

GUILLAUME: The way you act toward me is entirely unjust. Because, after all, you must know me well by now: I never had the military genius of my uncle;[25] I concerned myself with the Illuminists far more than I did with the French. If my soldiers did a bit of harm, they had as much done to them in return. And so, we are even: with as many casualties and injuries on both sides, everything is offset.

THE PRUSSIAN: See here the true feelings and language of a king. Monster! Here on this island you will pay for all the blood you spilled on the plains of Champagne, before Lille and Mayence.

A SPANISH SANS-CULOTTE: Behold his majesty the King of Spain.[26] He is very much of Bourbon blood: see here how stupidity, false piety, and despotism are imprinted on his royal face.

23. Frederick William II (1744–1797): the king of Prussia from 1786 to his death in 1797, he was drawn to mysticism and joined the occult Rosicrucian Order. Inspired by his faith and his Illuminist beliefs, he set out to protect Christianity from the threat of the Enlightenment, which had been supported by his predecessor, Frederick the Great—hence his defense plea in the play: "I concerned myself with the Illuminists far more than I did with the French." Truth be told, he also concerned himself with the French, since he participated in the military campaigns of 1792 and 1793 against the French republic.
24. George III, the king of England, who was also the Duke of Hanover.
25. Frederick the Great.
26. Charles IV (1748–1819): a member of the House of Bourbon (Spanish branch), Charles IV acceded to the throne in 1788 and endeavored to save the life of his cousin, Louis XVI. His diplomatic efforts having failed, he entered into armed conflict with the French republic in 1793 but lost the War of the Pyrenees.

CHARLES: I admit it, I'm only a fool who has always followed his wife and priests blindly; because of this, have mercy on me.

A NEAPOLITAN SANS-CULOTTE: Behold the crowned hypocrite of Naples.[27] A few more years, and he would have done more harm to Europe than Mount Vesuvius on his doorstep.

FERDINAND, KING OF NAPLES: Volcano for volcano, why didn't you just leave me there! I was the last one to enter the league. In the end I had no choice but to join forces with my brothers the kings. Can you really blame me for running with the pack?

A SARDINIAN SANS-CULOTTE: Here in this box lies his sleeping majesty Victor-Amédée-Marie de Savoie, king of the marmots.[28] More stupid than they, he once tried to play the villain, but we quickly put him back in his cage. Amédée, hurry up and sleep. I greatly fear that the volcano will not allow you to complete your six months of slumber.

THE KING OF SARDINIA, *getting out of his box, yawning, and rubbing his eyes*: I'm so hungry . . . Ah! Ah! Where is my chaplain to say grace?

THE SARDINIAN: Say *your graces* instead . . . Go! *(Pushing him.)* This is all they're good for, all these kings; drinking, eating, and sleeping, when they cannot do any harm.

---

27. Ferdinand IV (1751–1825): the king of Naples and of Sicily, he is a first cousin of Louis XVI and a brother-in-law of Marie-Antoinette, making him one of the fiercest enemies of the French Revolution.
28. Victor Amadeus III (1726–1796): the king of Sardinia, he was opposed to the French Revolution, opening his territories to the émigrés, refusing to welcome an embassy of the new republic, and waging a war against France, during which he would lose Nice and Savoy.

A RUSSIAN SANS-CULOTTE: *(CATHERINE walks onto the stage, taking great steps, great strides.)* Come now, you're putting on airs, I think . . . Behold her imperial majesty, the czarina of all the Russias,[29] also known as madam of the stride, or, if you prefer, the harlot, the Semiramis of the North:[30] a woman above her sex, for she never knew its virtues nor its modesty. Without morals and without shame, she murdered her husband, so as to have no companion on the throne, and never lack one in her impure bed.[31]

A POLISH SANS-CULOTTE: You, Stanislas-Auguste, King of Poland,[32] let's go, quickly! Carry the tail of your harlot mistress, whose lowly servant you so constantly were.

A SANS-CULOTTE, *holding in his hands the end of several chains attached to the necks of several KINGS:* Hold this! Here is the bottom of the barrel, the small fry who do not deserve the honor of being named.[33]

The OLD MAN serves as an interpreter for the SAVAGES, before whom the KINGS are paraded. He translates for them in the language of signs what is said as the KINGS appear onstage. One after the other, the SAVAGES give marks of astonishment and indignation.

29. Catherine II (1729–1796): she proclaimed herself the empress of Russia after having overthrown her husband. It is likely that she also had him assassinated, but this was never proven. The archetype of the enlightened despot, she admired and supported the Enlightenment but felt a deep aversion toward the French Revolution.
30. Maréchal recalls here, with biting irony, the nickname given to Catherine II by her many admirers, notably Voltaire.
31. A fifth passage cut during performances of the play, from "she murdered her husband" to "her impure bed."
32. Stanislas II Auguste (1732–1798): it is largely thanks to Catherine II, his former lover, that he was elected king of Poland. He would be its last king, after a turbulent reign.
33. Echoing, no doubt intentionally, one of Pierre Corneille's most famous lines: "Le reste ne vaut pas l'honneur d'être nommé" (The rest do not deserve the honor of being named). *Cinna,* act 5, scene 1.

A ROMAN SANS-CULOTTE, *leading the* POPE:[34] On your
knees, crowned scoundrels, so that you may receive the
blessing of the Holy Father: for there is only one priest
capable of absolving your crimes, of which he was the
accomplice and treacherous agent. Eh! In what despicable
plot did the priests and their leader not take part? In what
criminal scheme did they not play a role? It is this monster
with a triple crown who underhandedly launched a murderous crusade against the French, as his predecessors had
once advised one against the Saracens. Second only to
kings, the priests are those who did the most harm to the
world and to humanity.

Blessings, eternal blessings be given to the French
people, who first among the moderns recalled the patriotism of Brutus[35] and revealed the hypocrisy of oracles.
The French made the Romans blush for the incense they
prostituted at the feet of a priest in the Capitol, in the very
same spot where virtuous and republican hands had
stabbed the ambitious Caesar.

THE POPE: Ah! Ah! You paint too dark a picture . . . Name a
single one of my predecessors who showed as much mod-
eration as I did. Following their example, I could well have
placed a prohibition on the whole kingdom of France . . .

THE FRENCH SANS-CULOTTE, *interrupting him*: Say the
republic.

THE POPE: Well, the republic it is! The republic.

I could have called down the vengeance of heaven on
the heads of all Frenchmen, but I confined myself instead

---

34. Pope Pius VI (1717–1799): born Giovanni Angelico Braschi, he led the
Papal States from 1775 to his death in 1799.
35. Marcus Junius Brutus (ca. 85–42 B.C.): a Roman politician most
famous for his role in the assassination of Julius Caesar, after the latter
had made himself perpetual dictator. During the Revolution, his name
was synonymous with heroic resistance against tyranny.

to raising against them all the powers of the earth. Could a
priest do any less? Listen; have mercy on me, and for the
rest of my life I will pray to God for the sans-culottes.

THE ROMAN SANS-CULOTTE: No, no, no! We do not want
any more prayers from a priest: the God of the sans-culottes
is freedom; it is equality; it is fraternity! You have never
known and will never know these gods. Instead, go and
exorcise the volcano, which must soon punish you and
avenge us.

A FRENCH SANS-CULOTTE, *after having arranged all the
KINGS in a half circle, and before leaving them*: Crowned
monsters! You should have all died a thousand deaths on
the scaffold, but where could we have found executioners
who would have agreed to soil their hands with your vile
and corrupted blood? We leave you to your remorse, or
rather to your impotent rage.

And yet here are the authors of all our suffering! Future
generations, can you believe it! Here are those who held in
their hands and swayed Europe's destiny. It was for the
benefit of this handful of cowardly bandits, for the pleasure
of these crowned scoundrels, that the blood of one million,
of two million men, the worst of whom was still better
than they, was shed in almost all points of the continent
and across the seas. It was in the name or at the command
of these twenty ferocious animals that entire provinces
were destroyed, populous cities changed into a mound of
corpses and ashes, and countless families violated, left
naked, and exposed to famine. This odious group of
murderous politicians has led large nations to fail and has
turned against each other peoples made to be friends and
born to live as brothers. Here they are, these butchers of
men in times of war, these corrupters of humankind in
times of peace. It was from within the courts of these vile
beings that the contagion of all vices spread out to the

cities and countryside. Has there ever existed a nation that had a king and morals at the same time?

THE POPE: There weren't any morals in Rome! . . . Cardinals have no morals! . . .

THE FRENCH SANS-CULOTTE: And these ogres found eulogists and supporters! The priests only gave to their God the remains of the incense that they burned at the feet of princes. Slaves in golden liveries, they strutted and believed they were important when they said: *The king, my master* . . . [36] More than one hundred million men obeyed these dull tyrants and trembled when pronouncing their names with a saintly respect. It was to provide amusements to these man-eaters that the people, from dawn to dusk, and from the start of the year to its end, worked, sweated, and exhausted themselves. Future generations! Will you ever forgive your kind ancestors for this excess of degradation, stupidity, and self-denial? May nature hasten to complete the sans-culottes' work; may it blow its fiery breath on these dregs of society and forever return kings to the nothingness they never should have left.

May nature also return to the void the first among us who would pronounce the word *king* without adding the imprecations that the idea attached to this vile word naturally brings to any republican mind.

As for me, I vow to strike straight away from the book of free men anyone who in my presence would contaminate the air with an expression that would tend to make others look favorably on the king, or on any other monstrosity of this kind. Comrades, let us all swear it, and let us re-embark.

---

36. This is the sixth and final passage, extending from "Slaves in golden liveries" to "*my master,*" not to have been spoken onstage.

THE SANS-CULOTTES, *while leaving*: We swear it! . . . Long
live freedom! Long live the republic!

SCENE VI
The KINGS of Europe.

FRANÇOIS II: How they treat us, good God! With such
indignity! And what will become of us?

GUILLAUME: My dear Cagliostro;[37] why aren't you here?
You'd get us out of this mess.

GEORGE: I doubt it; what do you think, Holy Father? You've
been holding him prisoner in Castel Sant'Angelo[38] for a
long time.

BRASCHI, OR THE POPE: He couldn't help with any of this.
We need something supernatural.

THE KING OF SPAIN: Oh, Holy Father, a small miracle.

THE POPE: The time for it has passed . . . Where are the good
old days when saints flew through the air riding on a stick?

THE KING OF SPAIN: Oh Louis XVI! Oh my kin! You're still
the one who drew the best lot. You didn't have to suffer
long. Now you don't need anything anymore. Here we lack
everything: we are stuck between famine and hell. It is
you, François and Guillaume, who brought all this upon
us. I always knew that this French Revolution, sooner or

37. Count Alessandro di Cagliostro (1743–1795): the pseudonym of the
Italian occultist Joseph Balsamo who acquired great renown in the royal
courts of Europe. Implicated in the Affair of the Diamond Necklace, he
was incarcerated in the Bastille and banished from France before his
arrest by the Inquisition in 1789 for practicing freemasonry.
38. A fortress in Rome that served from the fourteenth to the nineteenth
centuries as a refuge for the popes in times of peril and as a tribunal and
prison of the Papal States. Cagliostro was imprisoned there by the
Inquisition.

later, would play a nasty trick on us. We shouldn't have intervened at all, not at all.

GUILLAUME: It suits you well, Lord of Spain, to accuse us. Was it not your ordinary slowness that caused our defeat? If you had supported us at the right moment, France would have been done for.

CATHERINE: As for me, I am going to sleep in this cave. Instead of arguing, may whoever love me follow me . . . Stanislas, won't you come keep me company?

THE KING OF POLAND: Old harlot, take a look at yourself in that stream.

CATHERINE: You haven't always been so proud.[39]

THE EMPEROR: Cursed French!

THE KING OF SPAIN: These sans-culottes whom we despised so much at first have nonetheless carried out their ambitions. Why didn't I have a beautiful auto-da-fé, to serve as an example for the others?

THE POPE: Why didn't I excommunicate them as early as 1789? We spared them too much, far too much.

THE KING OF NAPLES: These are all beautiful reflections, but they come a little late. When in a galley, one must row: before anything else, we must eat. Let us first worry about fishing, hunting, or plowing.

THE EMPEROR: It would be a fine thing to see the emperor of Austria toiling the earth to live.

THE KING OF SPAIN: Would you prefer we draw lots to determine which one of us will serve as food for the others?

---

39. Stanislas II was indeed Catherine II's lover in his youth and even owed her his crown.

THE POPE: We don't even have enough to perform the miracle of the multiplication of the loaves! This doesn't surprise me; there are schismatics[40] in our ranks.

CATHERINE: This accusation is clearly addressed to me: I demand satisfaction . . . En garde, Holy Father.

The EMPRESS and the POPE battle, one with her scepter and the other with his cross. A strike of the scepter shatters the cross; the POPE throws his tiara at CATHERINE's head and knocks off her crown. They fight using their chains. The KING OF POLAND attempts to put a stop to it by removing the scepter from CATHERINE's hands.

THE KING OF POLAND: Neighbor, that's enough. Easy! Easy!

THE EMPRESS: How fitting that you'd steal my scepter, coward! Is this to compensate for your own, which you allowed to be shattered into three or four pieces?[41]

THE POPE: Catherine, I ask for your mercy, *escolta mi*:[42] if you leave me be, I will absolve you of all your sins.

THE EMPRESS: Absolve me! You wretch of a priest! Before I leave you be, you must confess and repeat after me that a priest, that a pope, is but a charlatan, a swindler . . . Go on, repeat!

THE POPE: A priest . . . a pope . . . is but a charlatan . . . a swindler.

THE KING OF SPAIN, *to the side, in a corner of the stage*: What a find! I still have some bread left from the ration given to me in the hold of the ship. What treasure! No amount of

---

40. Anyone who secedes from a religious group and recognizes a different spiritual authority or dogma.
41. The expression "shattered into three or four pieces" refers to the second partition of Poland in 1793.
42. A likely mistake by Maréchal: the correct form should be *ascoltami* ("listen to me" in Italian).

rupees, no amount of piastres, are worth a piece of rye bread when one is dying of hunger.

THE KING OF POLAND: Cousin, what are you doing over there on your own? I believe you're eating, and I'd also like to partake.

The EMPRESS and the other KINGS throw themselves at their Spanish counterpart to wrest the morsel of bread from his grasp.

Me too, me too, and me too.

THE KING OF NAPLES: What would the sans-culottes say, if they saw all the kings of Europe squabbling over a morsel of rye bread?

The KINGS fight: the ground is littered with fragments of chains, scepters, and crowns; their coats are in tatters.

SCENE VII
The previous characters and the SANS-CULOTTES.

———

The SANS-CULOTTES, who had wished to enjoy from afar the predicament of the KINGS reduced to famine, return to the island to roll a barrel of crackers among the famished monarchs.

ONE OF THE SANS-CULOTTES, *smashing the barrel open and spilling the crackers*: There you go, you scoundrels, here's some food. Eat up. The proverb that says *Everyone must live* was not written for you, as there is no need for kings to live. But the sans-culottes are as prone to pity as they are to justice. So, feast on these crackers until you are acclimated to this country.

SCENE VIII

The KINGS throw themselves onto the crackers.

————

THE EMPRESS: One moment! As empress and owner of the largest territory, I must have the biggest share.

THE KING OF POLAND: Catherine never was a picky eater, but we are no longer in Saint Petersburg. Each gets his own.

THE KING OF NAPLES: Yes! Yes! Each gets his own. This barrel of crackers mustn't look like the so-called republic of Poland.

The KING OF PRUSSIA strikes the EMPRESS's fingers with his scepter.

THE EMPRESS: Be quiet, captor of Silesia.[43]

THE POPE: Gentlemen! Gentlemen! Render unto Caesar that which is Caesar's.

THE EMPRESS: And what if you were to render unto Caesar that which belongs to Caesar, little bishop of Rome! . . .

THE EMPEROR: That's enough, give it a rest! There's plenty for everyone.

THE KING OF PRUSSIA: Yes, but not for long.

THE KING OF NAPLES: Behold the volcano: it seems to want to put us all in agreement. Burning lava descends from the crater and moves toward us. Gods!

THE KING OF SPAIN: Our Blessed Lady! Save me . . . If I survive, I will become a sans-culotte.

---

43. Silesia is a region in central Europe mainly situated today in southwest Poland. Between 1740 and 1763, it was the object of numerous battles between Austria and Prussia. In the end, Prussia won the Silesian Wars and "captured" Silesia.

THE POPE: And I will take a wife.

CATHERINE: And I will join the Jacobins or the Cordeliers.[44]

The volcano begins its eruption: it throws rocks, burning coals, etc., onto the stage.

The explosion occurs: the fire besieges the KINGS from all sides; they fall, consumed within the bowels of the earth split asunder.

THE END

44. Catherine II refers here to two immensely influential and militant political societies, both affiliated, in 1793, with the Mountain: the Jacobin and the Cordeliers Clubs (each named after the former convent where it held its meetings).

Le Jugement dernier des rois

des rois

Prophétie en un acte, en prose,

PAR P. SYLVAIN MARÉCHAL,

JOUÉE *sur le Théâtre de la République, au mois Vendémiaire et jours suivants.*

———

TANDEM! . . .

———

A PARIS,
DE l'Imp. de C.-F. PATRIS, IMPRIMEUR
de la Com. rue du faubourg St.-Jacques, aux ci-devant
Dames Ste.-Marie.

———

L'AN second de la RÉPUBLIQUE FRANÇAISE,
une et indivisible.

AVIS
Aux directeurs de spectacles des départements.

———————

L'auteur, soussigné, se réserve les droits qu'un décret de la convention nationale lui maintient, sur les représentations de sa pièce, par les différents théâtres de la république.

Sylvain Maréchal

Nota. Les passages de la pièce, marqués de guillemets, ne se récitent pas au Théâtre.

L'IDÉE de cette pièce est prise dans l'Apologue suivant,
faisant partie des LEÇONS DU FILS AINÉ
D'UN ROI, ouvrage philosophique du même
auteur, publié au commencement de 1789,
et mis à l'INDEX par la Police.[1]

————

En ce temps-là: revenu de la cour, bien fatigué, un visionnaire[2] se livra au sommeil, et rêva que tous les peuples de la terre, le jour des Saturnales, se donnèrent le mot pour se saisir de la personne de leurs rois, chacun de son côté. Ils convinrent en même temps d'un rendez-vous général, pour rassembler cette poignée d'individus couronnés, et les reléguer dans une petite île inhabitée, mais habitable; le sol fertile n'attendait que des bras et une légère culture. On établit un cordon de petites chaloupes armées pour inspecter l'île, et empêcher ces nouveaux colons d'en sortir. L'embarras des nouveaux débarqués ne fut pas mince. Ils commencèrent par se dépouiller de tous leurs ornements royaux qui les embarrassaient; et il fallut que chacun, pour vivre, mît la

1. Signalons que cet apologue fut écrit et publié avant la Révolution. Si Maréchal renvoie ici à la deuxième édition de son livre, publiée à Bruxelles en 1789, la première date de 1788 et contient déjà le même apologue, intitulé "Vision. L'Ile déserte."

2. "Visionnaire" signifie, au dix-huitième siècle, une personne qui "croit faussement avoir des visions, des révélations" ou "qui a des idées folles, des imaginations extravagantes, des desseins chimériques" (*Dictionnaire de l'Académie française*, 1762). Il s'agit donc moins d'une personne qui a la prescience de l'avenir (définition moderne) que d'un aliéné.

main à la pâte. Plus de valets, plus de courtisans, plus de soldats. Il leur fallut tout faire par eux-mêmes. Cette cinquantaine de personnages ne vécut pas longtemps en paix; et le genre humain, spectateur tranquille, eut la satisfaction de se voir délivré de ses tyrans par leurs propres mains,—30 *et* 31 *pag.*

L'AUTEUR
DU
JUGEMENT DERNIER
DES ROIS,
AUX spectateurs de la première représentation de cette pièce.

————

CITOYENS, rappelez-vous donc comment, au temps passé, sur tous les théâtres on avilissait, on dégradait, on ridiculisait indignement les classes les plus respectables du peuple-souverain, pour faire rire les rois et leurs valets de cour. J'ai pensé qu'il était bien temps de leur rendre la pareille, et de nous en amuser à notre tour. Assez de fois ces *messieurs* ont eu les rieurs de leur côté; j'ai pensé que c'était le moment de les livrer à la risée publique, et de parodier ainsi un vers heureux de la comédie du méchant:

> Les rois sont ici bas pour nos menus plaisirs.

GRESSET.[3]

Voilà le motif des endroits un peu *chargés* du JUGEMENT DERNIER DES ROIS.

(Extrait du journal des *Révolutions de Paris*, de Prud'homme, Tome XVII, page 109, in-8°.)

———

3. Le vers provient en effet de la comédie *Le Méchant* de Jean-Baptiste-Louis Gresset, à un détail près (d'où la parodie): pour Gresset, "les sots sont ici-bas pour nos menus plaisirs" et non les rois (acte 2, scène 1). Telle était la popularité de la pièce de Gresset qu'un public du dix-huitième siècle aurait reconnu cette allusion et son assimilation des rois aux sots.

COSTUMES DES PERSONNAGES

L'IMPÉRATRICE: Corset de moire d'or, manches bouffantes; jupe de taffetas bleu, ornée d'un tour de point d'Espagne ou dentelle d'or; mante de satin ou taffetas ponceau, garnie au pourtour, ainsi que la jupe; tour de gorge de linon, formant la collerette; crachat attaché sur la césarine du manteau; couronne de paillons dorés; toque de taffetas bleu.

LE PAPE: Soutane et camail de laine, écarlate ou blanche; rochet de linon, entoilage de dentelle; gants blancs; souliers blancs avec une double croix en or sur le milieu du pied; tiare à trois couronnes, la tiare de satin ponceau et les couronnes en or; calotte de même satin, couvrant les oreilles, et bordée de poil blanc; étole et manipule.

LE ROI D'ESPAGNE: Habit espagnol, manteau, trousse, pantalon et les pièces de souliers, le tout rouge; un grand nez postiche en taffetas couleur de chair; couronne de moire d'or enrichie de pierreries; trois cordons en sautoir, savoir: un, ponceau, de l'ordre de la toison d'or; le deuxième, bleu de ciel avec une médaille; le troisième, de velours noir avec médaille.

L'EMPEREUR: Habit bleu galonné en or; cordon en sautoir, de l'ordre de l'Empire; un autre cordon blanc bordé de deux lignes rouges en bandoulière; écharpe ponceau, posée sur l'habit; couronne de moire d'or; veste, culotte et bas blancs.

LE ROI DE POLOGNE: Gilet à manches de velours noir; manteau à petites manches bouffantes de velours noir, de même que le gilet: il faut au manteau une armure de poil blanc; pantalon de tricot de soie cramoisie; cordon de l'ordre, de velours noir, brodé en or; un second cordon en bandoulière, bleu de ciel, avec un ordre quelconque.

LE ROI DE PRUSSE: Habit bleu foncé, boutonné jusqu'à la taille; grand chapeau à trois cornes; plumet et cocarde noirs; point d'Espagne en or autour du chapeau; culotte jaune; bottes à l'écuyère; coiffé en queue proche la tête; écharpe de satin blanc à frange d'or.

LE ROI D'ANGLETERRE: Habit bleu foncé avec des boutons d'or ou de cuivre; veste de même; ventre postiche pour le grossir; bottes à l'écuyère; jarretières de l'ordre *Honni soit qui mal y pense*, et un crachat du même ordre.

LE ROI DE NAPLES: Gilet espagnol à crevasses; chemisette de linon; trousse pareille au gilet; manteau espagnol, cordon ponceau avec une médaille en sautoir et un second cordon en sautoir, de velours noir, brodé en or.

LE ROI DE SARDAIGNE: Habit complet de Financier; cordon de l'ordre en sautoir; crachat attaché à l'habit; fronteau de couronne herminée.

UN SAUVAGE (rôle parlant):[4] Pantalon et gilet de tricot de soie, clairement tigrée; sandales lacées; perruque et barbe grises.

Huit SAUVAGES (personnages muets) carquois et flèches.

4. Hamiche affirme qu'il faut lire "le vieillard" et non "un sauvage" (Hamiche, *Le Théâtre et la Révolution*, 306). Il est vrai que le costume décrit semble plus conforme au vieillard qu'à un sauvage (et pourquoi un seul sauvage et pas les autres?), et qu'il est surprenant que le vieillard ne soit pas inclus dans cette liste de personnages. En outre, aucun des sauvages n'a de "rôle parlant," à l'inverse, bien entendu, du vieillard. Cela dit, pourquoi préciser que le vieillard a un rôle parlant sans faire de même pour tous les autres personnages, notamment les sans-culottes et les rois? Cette précision ne suggère-t-elle pas une tentative de différencier un sauvage des autres qui sont d'ailleurs décrits tout de suite après comme des "personnages muets"? Le mystère reste complet.

Dix SANS-CULOTTES portant le costume du pays de chacun des Rois qu'ils amènent enchaînés par le col, c'est-à-dire un Sans-Culotte Espagnol, Allemand, Italien, Napolitain, Polonais, Prussien, Russe, Sarde, Anglais, et un Français.

Un grand nombre de Peuple armé de sabres, fusils et piques, tous habillés en Sans-Culottes Français.

Une Barrique remplie de Biscuit de mer.

PERSONNAGES

UN VIEILLARD FRANÇAIS. . . . . *Monvel.*

DES SAUVAGES de tout âge et de tout sexe.

UN SANS-CULOTTE de chaque nation de l'Europe.

LES ROIS D'EUROPE, y compris

LE PAPE. . . . . *Dugazon.*

ET LA CZARINE. . . . . *Michot.*[5]

L'EMPEREUR. . . . . *Raymont.*

LE ROI D'ANGLETERRE.

LE ROI DE PRUSSE.

LE ROI DE NAPLES.

LE ROI D'ESPAGNE. . . . . *Baptiste le jeune.*

LE ROI DE SARDAIGNE.

LE ROI DE POLOGNE. *Grand-Mesnil.*

5. Notons que pour ajouter au ridicule du personnage, le rôle de Catherine II était tenu par un homme, le célèbre acteur comique Antoine Michaut, dit Michot.

LE JUGEMENT DERNIER DES ROIS, PROPHÉTIE EN UN ACTE

Le théâtre représente l'intérieur d'une île à moitié volcanisée. Dans *la profondeur, ou arrière-scène, une montagne jette des flammèches de temps à autre pendant toute l'action jusqu'à la fin. Sur un des côtés de l'avant-scène, quelques arbres ombragent une cabane abritée derrière par un grand rocher blanc, sur lequel on lit cette inscription, tracée avec du charbon:*

> Il vaut mieux avoir pour voisin
> Un volcan qu'un roi.
> Liberté. . . . Égalité.

Au-dessous sont plusieurs chiffres. Un ruisseau tombe en cascade, et coule sur le côté de la chaumière.

De l'autre part, la vue de la mer.

Le soleil se lève derrière le rocher blanc pendant le monologue du VIEILLARD, *qui ajoute un chiffre à ceux déjà tracés par lui.*

SCÈNE PREMIÈRE

LE VIEILLARD: *(Il compte.)* 1, 2, 3 . . . 19, 20. Voilà donc précisément aujourd'hui vingt ans que je suis relégué dans cette île déserte. Le despote qui a signé mon bannissement est peut-être mort à présent . . . [6] Là-bas, dans ma pauvre patrie,

---

6. De quel despote s'agit-il? La question est plus complexe qu'il n'y paraît. Déduire vingt années de la date de la première représentation de la pièce situerait le bannissement du vieillard en automne 1773, sous le règne de

on me croit brûlé par le volcan, ou déchiré sous la dent de quelques bêtes féroces, ou mangé par des anthropophages. Le volcan, les animaux carnassiers, les sauvages, semblent avoir respecté jusqu'à ce jour la victime d'un roi . . . Mes bons amis tardent bien à venir: le soleil est pourtant levé! . . . Qu'est-ce que j'aperçois? . . . Ce ne sont pas leurs canots ordinaires . . . Une chaloupe! . . . Elle approche à force de rames. Des blancs . . . des Européens! . . . Si c'étaient de mes compatriotes, des Français . . . Ils viennent peut-être me chercher . . . Le tyran sera mort; et son successeur, pour se populariser, comme cela se pratique à tous les avènements au trône, aura fait grâce à quelques victimes innocentes du règne précédent . . . Je ne veux point de la clémence d'un despote: je resterai, je mourrai dans cette île volcanisée, plutôt que de retourner sur le continent, du moins tant qu'il y aura des rois et des prêtres.

Caché derrière cette roche, il faut que je sache à qui tout ce monde en veut ici.

Louis XV. Truchet rejette toutefois cette hypothèse, car il serait selon lui absurde de penser que Maréchal souhaitait s'en prendre à Marie Leszczynska et non à Marie-Antoinette dans les passages où le vieillard blâme la reine. C'est oublier, observe-t-il, que la pièce est une prophétie: "l'action se joue dans le futur, après la victoire totale de la République sur les rois; or il suffisait d'attendre le mois de mai 1794 pour que le souverain régnant vingt ans plus tôt devînt Louis XVI, et la reine Marie-Antoinette." Truchet, *Théâtre du XVIIIe siècle*, 1561–1562.

SCÈNE II

Douze ou quinze SANS-CULOTTES,[7] un de chaque nation de l'Europe. *(Ils débarquent.)*

————

LE SANS-CULOTTE FRANÇAIS: Voyons si cette île fera notre affaire. C'est la troisième que nous visitons: elle paraît avoir été volcanisée, et l'être encore. Tant mieux! Le globe sera plus tôt débarrassé de tous les brigands couronnés dont on nous a confié la déportation.

L'ANGLAIS: Il me semble qu'ils seront fort bien ici. La main de la nature s'empressera de ratifier, de sanctionner le jugement porté par les sans-culottes contre les rois, ces scélérats si longtemps privilégiés et impunis.

L'ESPAGNOL: Qu'ils éprouvent ici tous les tourments de l'enfer, auquel ils ne croyaient pas, et qu'ils nous faisaient prêcher par les prêtres, leurs complices, pour nous *embêter.*[8]

LE FRANÇAIS: Camarades! Cette île paraît habitée . . . Remarquez-vous ces pas d'hommes?

LE SARDE: À l'entrée de cette caverne, voilà des fruits tout fraîchement récoltés.

LE FRANÇAIS: Mes amis! Venez, hé! Venez donc; lisez:

Il vaut mieux avoir pour voisin
Un volcan qu'un roi.

PLUSIEURS SANS-CULOTTES, *ensemble*: Bravo! Bravo!

————

7. Les sans-culottes, nommés ainsi parce qu'ils ne portaient pas la culotte courte des nobles et des bourgeois, étaient des révolutionnaires issus du petit peuple. Prônant une démocratie directe et une société plus égalitaire, ils ont exercé une grande influence sur la vie politique, particulièrement entre 1792 et 1794, à travers leur participation dans les clubs patriotiques, les pétitions qu'ils formulaient dans les sections de Paris et qu'ils présentaient aux assemblées législatives, et le recours à la violence populaire (ou à la menace d'une telle violence).

8. "Embêter" signifie, au dix-huitième siècle, "rendre stupide, aveugler." *Littré*, 1873.

LE FRANÇAIS, *continue de lire*:

> *Liberté. . . . Égalité.*

Il y a ici quelque martyr de l'ancien régime. L'heureuse rencontre!

L'ANGLAIS: Oh! Que nous avons bien adressé! Celui qui gémit en ce lieu ne s'attend pas à trouver aujourd'hui des libérateurs.

LE FRANÇAIS: L'infortuné ne sait rien: il serait mort, sans apprendre la liberté de son pays.

L'ALLEMAND: Et de toute l'Europe. Il ne doit pas être loin: cherchons-le; allons au-devant de lui.

LE FRANÇAIS: Qu'il me tarde de le rencontrer! C'est sans doute un des nôtres; et, à en juger d'après les saints noms qu'il a tracés sur cette roche, il est digne de la grande Révolution, puisqu'il a su la pressentir à ce bout du monde.

SCÈNE III
Les acteurs précédents et LE VIEILLARD.

————

PLUSIEURS SANS-CULOTTES, *à la fois*: Bon vieillard! . . . Vénérable vieillard! . . . Que fais-tu ici?

LE VIEILLARD: Des Français! . . . Ô jour heureux! . . . Il y a si longtemps que je n'ai vu des Français! . . . Mes amis! Mes enfants! Que cherchez-vous? . . . Mais avant tout, un naufrage vous a peut-être jetés sur cette rive; auriez-vous besoin de nourriture? Je n'ai à vous offrir que ces fruits, et l'eau de cette source. Ma cabane est trop petite pour vous contenir tous à la fois. Je n'attendais pas si nombreuse et si bonne compagnie.

LE FRANÇAIS: Notre bon papa, il ne nous faut rien. Nous n'avons besoin que de t'entendre, de savoir ton histoire; nous te raconterons, après, la nôtre.

LE VIEILLARD: En deux mots, la voici: je suis français, né à Paris. J'habitais un petit domaine contre le parc de Versailles. Un jour, la chasse passe de mon côté; le cerf est relancé jusque dans mon jardin. Le roi et tout son monde entrent chez moi.[9] Ma fille, grande et belle, est remarquée de tous ces *messieurs* de la cour. Le lendemain, on me l'enlève . . . Je cours au château réclamer ma fille; on me raille: on me repousse: on me chasse. Je ne me rebute pas: la larme à l'œil, je me jette aux pieds du roi sur son passage. On lui dit un mot à l'oreille sur mon compte; il me ricane au nez, et donne ordre qu'on me fasse retirer. Ma pauvre femme n'en obtient pas davantage; elle expire de douleur. Je reviens au château. Je conte ma peine à tout le monde. Personne ne veut s'en mêler. Je demande à parler à la reine; je la saisis par la robe, comme elle sortait de ses appartements. Ah! dit-elle, c'est cet ennuyeux personnage. Quand donc lui interdira-t-on ma présence?[10] Je me présente chez les ministres, j'élève le ton; je parle en homme, en père. Un d'eux, c'était un prélat, ne me répond rien; mais il fait un signe. On m'arrête à la porte de son audience; on me plonge dans un cachot, d'où je ne sors que pour être jeté à fond de cale d'un navire qui, en passant, me laissa dans cette île, il y a précisément aujourd'hui vingt années. Voilà, mes amis, mon aventure.

LE SANS-CULOTTE FRANÇAIS: Écoute à ton tour, et apprends que tu es bien vengé. Te dire tout serait trop long. Voici l'essentiel: Bon vieillard! Tu as devant toi un représentant

9. L'histoire du vieillard constitue une réécriture inversée de *La Partie de chasse de Henri IV,* pièce royaliste de Charles Collé qui avait connu beaucoup de succès au début de la Révolution française. Pour en savoir plus, lire la section "A Parodic Imagination" dans l'introduction de cette édition.
10. Une note au début de l'édition indique que "les passages de la pièce, marqués de guillemets, ne se récitent pas au Théâtre." Le premier passage à ne pas avoir été prononcé sur scène s'étend de "Je demande à parler" jusqu'à "ma présence."

de chacune des nations de l'Europe devenue libre et républicaine: car il faut que tu saches qu'il n'y a plus du tout de rois en Europe.

LE VIEILLARD: Est-il bien vrai? Serait-il possible? . . . Vous vous jouez d'un pauvre vieillard.

LE SANS-CULOTTE FRANÇAIS: De vrais sans-culottes honorent la vieillesse, et ne s'en amusent point . . . comme faisaient jadis les plats courtisans de Versailles, de Saint-James, de Madrid, de Vienne.

LE VIEILLARD: Comment! Il n'y a plus de rois en Europe? . . .

UN SANS-CULOTTE: Tu vas les voir débarquer tous ici; ils nous suivent (à leur tour, comme tu l'as été) à fond de cale d'une petite frégate armée que nous devançons pour leur préparer les logis. Tu vas les voir tous ici, un pourtant excepté.

LE VIEILLARD: Et pourquoi cette exception? Ils n'ont jamais guère mieux valu les uns que les autres.

LE SANS-CULOTTE: Tu as raison . . . *excepté un*, parce que nous l'avons guillotiné.

LE VIEILLARD: *Guillotiné*! . . . Que veut dire? . . .

LE SANS-CULOTTE: Nous t'expliquerons cela, et bien autre chose[11]: nous lui avons tranché la tête, de par la loi.

LE VIEILLARD: Les Français sont donc devenus des hommes!

LE SANS-CULOTTE: Des hommes libres. En un mot, la France est une république dans toute la force du terme . . . Le peuple français s'est levé. Il a dit: *je ne veux plus de roi*; et le trône a disparu. Il a dit encore: *je veux la république*, et nous voilà tous républicains.

---

11. Second passage non-récité, de "Tu as raison" jusqu'à "autre chose."

LE VIEILLARD: Je n'aurais jamais osé espérer une pareille
révolution: mais je la conçois. J'avais toujours pensé, à part
moi, que le peuple, aussi puissant que le Dieu qu'on lui
prêche, n'a qu'à vouloir . . . Que je suis heureux d'avoir
assez vécu pour apprendre un aussi grand évènement! Ah!
Mes amis! Mes frères, mes enfants! Je suis dans un
ravissement! . . .

Mais jusqu'à présent vous ne me parlez que de la France;
et, ce me semble, si j'ai bien entendu d'abord, l'Europe
entière est délivrée de la contagion des rois?

L'ALLEMAND: L'exemple des Français a fructifié: ce n'a pas été
sans peine. Toute l'Europe s'est liguée contre eux, non pas
les peuples, mais les monstres qui s'en disaient impudem-
ment les *souverains*. Ils ont armé tous leurs esclaves; ils ont
mis en œuvre tous les moyens pour dissoudre ce noyau de
liberté que Paris avait formé. On a d'abord indignement
calomnié cette nation généreuse qui, la première, a fait
justice de son roi: on a voulu la modérantiser,[12] la
fédéraliser, l'affamer, l'asservir de plus belle, pour dégoûter
à jamais les hommes du régime de l'indépendance. Mais à
force de méditer les principes sacrés de la Révolution
française, à force de lire les traits sublimes, les vertus
héroïques auxquelles elle a donné lieu, les autres peuples se
sont dit: Mais, nous sommes bien dupes de nous laisser
conduire à la boucherie comme des moutons, ou de nous
laisser mener en laisse comme des chiens de chasse au
combat du taureau. Fraternisons plutôt avec nos aînés en
raison, en liberté. En conséquence, chaque section de
l'Europe envoya à Paris de braves sans-culottes, chargés de
la représenter. Là, dans cette diète de tous les peuples, on
est convenu qu'à certain jour, toute l'Europe se lèverait

---

12. Verbe dérivé de "modérantisme," terme péjoratif employé pendant la
Révolution française par les Montagnards et autres partis de gauche pour
décrire leurs homologues plus modérés.

en masse . . . et s'émanciperait . . . En effet, une insurrection générale et simultanée a éclaté chez toutes les nations
de l'Europe; et chacune d'elles eut son 14 juillet et 5 octobre
1789, son 10 août et 21 septembre 1792, son 31 mai et 2 juin
1793.[13] Nous t'instruirons de ces époques, les plus éton-
nantes de toute l'histoire.

LE VIEILLARD: Que de merveilles! . . . Pour le moment,
satisfaites mon impatiente curiosité sur un seul point. Je
vous entends tous répéter le mot de *sans-culotte*; que signifie
cette expression singulière et piquante?

LE SANS-CULOTTE FRANÇAIS: C'est à moi de te le dire: un
sans-culotte est un homme libre, un patriote par excellence.
La masse du vrai peuple, toujours bonne, toujours saine, est
composée de sans-culottes. Ce sont des citoyens purs, tout
près du besoin, qui mangent leur pain à la sueur de leur
front, qui aiment le travail, qui sont bons fils, bons pères,
bons époux, bons parents, bons amis, bons voisins, mais
qui sont jaloux de leurs droits autant que de leurs devoirs.
Jusqu'à ce jour, faute de s'entendre, ils n'avaient été que des
instruments aveugles et passifs dans la main des méchants,
c'est-à-dire des rois, des nobles, des prêtres, des égoïstes,
des aristocrates, des hommes d'état, des fédéralistes, tous
gens dont nous t'expliquerons, sage et malheureux vieillard,
les maximes et les forfaits. Chargés de tout l'entretien de la
ruche, les sans-culottes ne veulent plus souffrir désormais,

---

13. Le sans-culotte allemand énumère ici plusieurs grandes journées de la
Révolution française: la prise de la Bastille (14 juillet 1789), la marche des
femmes et de la garde nationale sur Versailles (5 et 6 octobre 1789), la
prise des Tuileries, la suspension du roi, et la création de la Convention
nationale (10 août 1792), l'abolition de la monarchie et la proclamation
de la république par cette même Convention (21 septembre 1792), et
l'insurrection qui entraîna la perte de pouvoir des Girondins au profit des
Montagnards, devenus maîtres de la Convention (31 mai et 2 juin 1793).

au-dessus ni parmi eux, de frelons lâches et malfaisants, orgueilleux et parasites.[14]

LE VIEILLARD, *avec enthousiasme*: Mes frères, mes enfants, et moi aussi je suis un sans-culotte!

L'ANGLAIS, *reprend le récit*: Chaque peuple, le même jour, s'est donc déclaré en république, et se constitua un gouvernement libre. Mais en même temps on proposa d'organiser une *convention Européenne* qui se tint à Paris, chef-lieu de l'Europe. Le premier acte qu'on y proclama fut le Jugement dernier des Rois détenus déjà dans les prisons de leurs châteaux. Ils ont été condamnés à la déportation dans une île déserte, où ils seront gardés à vue sous l'inspection et la responsabilité d'une petite flotte que chaque république à son tour entretiendra en croisière jusqu'à la mort du dernier de ces monstres.[15]

LE VIEILLARD: Mais, dites-moi, je vous prie, pourquoi vous être donné la peine d'amener tous ces rois jusqu'ici? Il eût été plus expédient de les pendre tous, à la même heure, sous le portique de leurs palais.

LE SANS-CULOTTE FRANÇAIS: Non, non! Leur supplice eût été trop doux et aurait fini trop tôt: il n'eût pas rempli le but qu'on se proposait. Il a paru plus convenable d'offrir à l'Europe le spectacle de ses tyrans détenus dans une ménagerie et se dévorant les uns les autres, ne pouvant plus assouvir leur rage sur les braves sans-culottes qu'ils osaient appeler leurs *sujets*. Il est bon de leur donner le loisir de se reprocher réciproquement leurs forfaits, et de se punir de leurs propres mains. Tel est le jugement solennel et en dernier ressort qui a été prononcé contre

---

14. Reprise probable d'une métaphore employée par Jacques Hébert dans son journal *Le Père Duchesne*. *Le Père Duchesne*, numéro 14, 1790.
15. Troisième passage supprimé à la représentation, de "Chaque peuple" jusqu'à "ces monstres."

eux à l'unanimité, et que nous venons sur ces mers mettre à exécution.

LE VIEILLARD: Je me rends.

UN SANS-CULOTTE: À présent que te voilà à-peu-près au fait, dis-nous, bon vieillard, cette île que tu habites depuis vingt ans, te semblerait-elle propre à y déposer notre cargaison de mauvaise marchandise?

LE VIEILLARD: Mes amis, cette île n'est point habitée. Quand j'y fus jeté, c'était le matin; je ne rencontrai aucun être vivant dans tout le cours de la journée; le soir, une pirogue vint mouiller à cette petite rade. Il en sortit plusieurs familles de sauvages, dont j'eus peur d'abord. Je ne leur rendais pas justice: ils dissipèrent bientôt mes craintes par un accueil hospitalier, et me promirent de m'apporter chaque soir de leur fruit, de leur chasse ou de leur pêche: car ils venaient tous les jours, à l'entrée de la nuit, dans cette île, pour y rendre un culte religieux au volcan que vous voyez. Sans contrarier leur croyance, je les invitai à partager du moins leurs hommages entre le volcan et le soleil. Ils ne manquèrent pas de revenir de grand matin, le troisième jour suivant, pour y voir le phénomène que je leur avais annoncé, et auquel ils n'avaient point fait attention dans leurs huttes enfumées. Je les plaçai sur ce rocher blanc; je leur fis contempler le lever du soleil sortant de la mer dans toute sa pompe: ce spectacle les tint dans l'extase. Depuis ce moment, il n'est pas de semaine qu'ils ne viennent adorer le soleil levant.[16] Depuis ce moment aussi, ils me regardent et me traitent comme leur père, leur médecin, leur conseil; et, grâce à eux, je ne manque de rien dans cette solitude inculte. Une fois, ils voulaient à toute force me reconnaître pour leur

16. Plusieurs phrases, de "Sans contrarier leur croyance" à "le soleil levant," furent sautées lors des représentations.

roi: je leur expliquai le mieux qu'il me fut possible mon aventure de là-bas, et ils jurèrent entre mes mains de n'avoir jamais de rois, pas plus que de prêtres.[17]

J'estime que cette île remplira parfaitement vos intentions; d'autant mieux, que depuis quelques semaines le cratère du volcan s'élargit beaucoup, et semble menacer d'une éruption prochaine. Il vaut mieux qu'elle éclate sur des têtes couronnées que sur celles de mes bons voisins les sauvages, ou de mes frères les braves sans-culottes.

UN SANS-CULOTTE: Camarades, qu'en dites-vous? Je crois qu'il a raison: signalons la flotte pour qu'elle vienne nous joindre ici, et qu'elle y vomisse les poisons dont elle est chargée.

LE VIEILLARD: J'aperçois mes bons voisins; abaissez vos piques devant eux en signe de fraternité; vous les verrez déposer leurs armes à vos pieds. Je ne sais point leur langue; ils ignorent la nôtre: mais le cœur est de tous les pays: nous nous entretenons par gestes, et nous nous comprenons parfaitement.

Des familles SAUVAGES sortent de leurs pirogues. LE VIEILLARD les présente aux SANS-CULOTTES d'Europe. On fraternise; on s'embrasse: LE VIEILLARD monte sur son rocher blanc, et fait hommage au soleil des fruits que lui ont apportés les SAUVAGES, dans des paniers d'osier adroitement travaillés.

Après la cérémonie, LE VIEILLARD converse avec eux par gestes et les met au courant.

Les ROIS débarquent: ils entrent sur la scène un à un, le sceptre à la main, le manteau royal sur les épaules, la couronne d'or sur la tête, et au cou une longue chaîne de fer dont un SANS-CULOTTE tient le bout.

17. Sans doute y a-t-il là un écho du célèbre apologue des Troglodytes de Montesquieu qui se termine sur la scène d'un bon vieillard refusant de devenir roi. *Lettres persanes*, lettre 14.

SCÈNE IV
Les précédents, familles SAUVAGES.

————

LE VIEILLARD: Braves sans-culottes, ces sauvages sont nos aînés en liberté: car ils n'ont jamais eu de rois. Nés libres, ils vivent et meurent comme ils sont nés.[18]

SCÈNE V
Les précédents, les ROIS d'Europe.

————

UN SANS-CULOTTE ALLEMAND, *conduisant l'empereur qui ouvre la marche*: Place à sa majesté l'empereur[19] . . . Il ne lui a manqué que du temps et plus de génie pour consommer tous les forfaits commis par la maison d'Autriche, et pour porter à leur comble les maux que Joseph II[20] et Antoinette voulaient, et firent à la France. Fléau de ses voisins, il le fut encore de son pays, dont il épuisa la population et les finances. Il fit languir l'agriculture, entrava le commerce, enchaîna la pensée. *(En secouant sa chaîne.)* N'ayant pu avoir le principal lot dans le partage de la Pologne, il voulut s'en dédommager en ravageant les frontières d'une nation dont il redoutait les lumières et l'énergie. Faux ami, allié perfide, faisant le mal pour mal faire; c'est un monstre.

FRANÇOIS II: Pardonnez-moi; je ne suis pas aussi monstre qu'on paraît le croire. Il est vrai que la Lorraine me tentait:

18. Allusion probable à une phrase célèbre du *Contrat social* de Jean-Jacques Rousseau: "L'homme est né libre, et partout il est dans les fers."
19. François II (1768–1835): empereur du Saint-Empire romain germanique, neveu de Marie-Antoinette, François II passe les vingt-deux premières années de son règne, de 1792 à 1814, en guerre contre la France, y perdant une grande partie de ses titres et de ses possessions.
20. Joseph II (1741–1790): empereur du Saint-Empire romain germanique de 1765 à 1790, il est le frère de Marie-Antoinette et l'oncle de François II. Souverain réformiste inspiré par l'esprit des Lumières, il n'apparaît pas dans la pièce de Maréchal puisque déjà mort en 1793.

mais la France n'eût-elle pas été trop heureuse d'acheter la paix et le bon ordre au prix d'une province? N'en a-t-elle pas déjà assez? D'ailleurs, s'il y a quelqu'un à blâmer, c'est le vieux Kaunitz qui abusa de ma jeunesse, de mon inexpérience: c'est Cobourg, c'est Brunswick.[21]

L'ALLEMAND: *(Il le lâche.)* Dis, ta vilaine âme, ton mauvais cœur . . . Achève ici de vivre, séparé à jamais de l'espèce humaine, dont toi et tes confrères avez fait trop longtemps la honte et le supplice.

UN SANS-CULOTTE ANGLAIS, *menant le ROI D'ANGLETERRE en laisse avec une chaîne:* Voici sa majesté le roi d'Angleterre,[22] qui, aidé du génie machiavélique de M. Pitt,[23] pressura la bourse du peuple anglais, et accrut encore le fardeau de la dette publique pour organiser en France la guerre civile, l'anarchie, la famine, et le fédéralisme, pire que tout cela.

GEORGE: Mais je n'avais pas la tête à moi, vous le savez. Punit-on un fou? On le place à l'hôpital.

L'ANGLAIS, *en le lâchant:* Le volcan te rendra la raison.

---

21. François II blâme ici Wenceslas Antoine de Kaunitz (1711–1794), chancelier de cour et d'État des Habsbourg; Frédéric Josias de Saxe-Cobourg-Saalfeld (1737–1815), commandant en chef de l'armée impériale; et Charles-Guillaume-Ferdinand de Brunswick-Wolfenbüttel (1735–1806), Generalfeldmarschall commandant les troupes coalisées de la Prusse et de l'Autriche.

22. George III (1738–1820): roi de Grande-Bretagne de 1760 à sa mort en 1820, son règne fut marqué de nombreuses guerres, dont la plupart l'opposaient à la France (guerre de Sept Ans et guerres successives contre la France révolutionnaire et napoléonienne). Avant même le début de la Révolution, il est notoire qu'il souffre de troubles psychiatriques.

23. William Pitt le Jeune (1759–1806): premier ministre de Grande-Bretagne, grand ennemi de la Révolution, il conclut des alliances contre la France et y fomente des troubles civils. En 1793, il fait d'ailleurs l'objet d'un décret de la Convention nationale le déclarant "ennemi du genre humain."

UN SANS-CULOTTE PRUSSIEN: Voici sa majesté le roi de Prusse:[24] comme le duc d'Hanovre,[25] bête malfaisante et sournoise, la dupe des charlatans, le bourreau des gens de bien et des hommes libres.

GUILLAUME: La manière dont vous en agissez envers moi est de toute injustice. Car enfin vous devez me connaître: je n'ai jamais eu le génie militaire de mon oncle;[26] je m'occupai beaucoup plus des Illuminés que des Français. Si mes soldats ont fait un peu de mal, on le leur a bien rendu. Ainsi quitte: tant de tués que de blessés, de part et d'autre, tout est compensé.

LE PRUSSIEN: Voilà bien les sentiments et le langage d'un roi. Monstre! Expie ici tout le sang que tu as fait verser dans les plaines de la Champagne, devant Lille et Mayence.

UN SANS-CULOTTE ESPAGNOL: Voici sa majesté le roi d'Espagne.[27] Il est bien du sang des Bourbons: voyez comme la sottise, la cagoterie[28] et le despotisme sont empreints sur sa face royale.

24. Frédéric-Guillaume II (1744–1797): roi de Prusse de 1786 jusqu'à sa mort, il est attiré par le mysticisme et rejoint l'ordre occulte des Rose-Croix. Inspiré par sa foi et ses croyances illuministes, il s'évertue à protéger la religion chrétienne qu'il croit menacée par les Lumières de son prédécesseur, Frédéric II, d'où sa plaidoirie dans la pièce: "je m'occupai beaucoup plus des Illuminés que des Français." Notons cependant qu'il s'occupa également des Français, puisqu'il participa aux campagnes de 1792 et 1793 contre la République française.
25. George III, le roi d'Angleterre, qui était également le duc de Hanovre.
26. Frédéric II de Prusse, dit Frédéric le Grand.
27. Charles IV (1748–1819): membre de la Maison de Bourbon (branche d'Espagne), Charles IV accède au trône en 1788 et s'évertue à sauver la vie de Louis XVI, son cousin. Ses efforts diplomatiques s'étant soldés par un échec, il entre en conflit armé avec la France républicaine en 1793 mais perd la Guerre du Roussillon.
28. Dévotion excessive, hypocrite.

CHARLES: J'en conviens, je ne suis qu'un sot, que les prêtres et ma femme ont toujours mené par le bout du nez; ainsi, faites-moi grâce.

UN SANS-CULOTTE NAPOLITAIN: Voici l'hypocrite couronné de Naples.[29] Encore quelques années, et il eût fait plus de ravage en Europe que le mont Vésuve qu'il avait à sa porte.

FERDINAND, ROI DE NAPLES: Volcan pour volcan, que ne me laissiez-vous là-bas! J'ai été le dernier à me mettre de la ligue. Il a bien fallu à la fin que je me rangeasse du parti de mes confrères les rois. Ne fallait-il pas hurler avec les loups?

UN SANS-CULOTTE SARDE: Voici dans cette boîte sa majesté dormeuse Victor-Amédée-Marie de Savoie, roi des marmottes.[30] Plus stupide qu'elles, une fois il a voulu faire le méchant; mais nous l'avons bien vite remis dans sa loge. Amédée, dépêche-toi de dormir. J'ai bien peur pour toi que le volcan ne te permette pas d'achever tes six mois de sommeil.

LE ROI DE SARDAIGNE, *sortant de sa boîte, bâillant et se frottant les yeux*: J'ai faim, moi . . . Ah! Ah! Où est mon chapelain pour dire mon *Benedicite*?[31]

LE SARDE: Dis plutôt *tes grâces* . . . Va! *(En le poussant.)* Voilà à quoi ils sont bons, tous ces rois; boire, manger, dormir, quand ils ne peuvent faire du mal.

29. Ferdinand IV (1751–1825): roi de Naples et de Sicile, il est cousin germain de Louis XVI et beau-frère de Marie-Antoinette, faisant de lui un des plus âpres ennemis de la Révolution.
30. Victor-Amédée III (1726–1796): roi de Sardaigne, il s'oppose à la Révolution, ouvrant ses territoires aux émigrés, refusant de recevoir l'ambassade de la République française, et menant contre la France une guerre au cours de laquelle il perdra le duché de Savoie et le comté de Nice.
31. Prière que font les chrétiens avant le repas.

UN SANS-CULOTTE RUSSE: *(CATHERINE monte sur la scène, en faisant de grands pas, de grandes enjambées.)* Allons donc, tu fais des façons, je crois . . . Voici sa majesté impériale, la Czarine de toutes les Russies;[32] autrement, madame de l'enjambée; ou, si vous aimez mieux, la Catau, la Sémiramis du Nord:[33] femme au-dessus de son sexe, car elle n'en connut jamais les vertus ni la pudeur. Sans mœurs et sans vergogne, elle fut l'assassin de son mari, pour n'avoir pas de compagnon sur le trône, et pour n'en pas manquer dans son lit impur.[34]

UN SANS-CULOTTE POLONAIS: Toi, Stanislas-Auguste, roi de Pologne,[35] allons, vite! Porte la queue de ta maîtresse Catau, dont tu fus si constamment le bas-valet.

UN SANS-CULOTTE, *tenant à la main le bout de plusieurs chaînes attachées au cou de plusieurs ROIS:* Tenez! Voici le fond du sac. C'est le fretin:[36] il ne vaut pas l'honneur d'être nommé.[37]

LE VIEILLARD sert de truchement aux SAUVAGES, devant lesquels passent en revue les ROIS. Il leur traduit dans le langage des signes ce

32. Catherine II (1729–1796): elle se fit proclamer impératrice de Russie après avoir fomenté un coup d'état contre son mari. Il est probable qu'elle le fit aussi assassiner mais cela ne fut jamais prouvé. Archétype du despote éclairé, elle admira et soutint les Lumières mais ressentit une aversion profonde à l'égard de la Révolution.
33. Maréchal reprend ici de manière ironique le surnom donné à Catherine II par ses nombreux admirateurs, dont Voltaire.
34. Cinquième passage à ne pas avoir été recité au théâtre, de "elle fut l'assassin" à "son lit impur."
35. Stanislas II Auguste (1732–1798): c'est en grande partie grâce à Catherine II, son ancienne amante, qu'il sera élu roi de Pologne en 1764. Il en sera le dernier roi, après un règne très mouvementé.
36. Surtout employé aujourd'hui dans l'expression pléonastique "menu fretin," le mot "fretin" se dit des petits poissons que les pêcheurs rejettent à l'eau et, au figuré, des choses de rebut ou des gens de petite condition dont on fait peu de cas.
37. Rappel sans doute délibéré du célèbre vers de Pierre Corneille: "Le reste ne vaut pas l'honneur d'être nommé." *Cinna*, acte 5, scène 1.

qui se dit à mesure que les ROIS *paraissent sur la scène. Les* SAUVAGES *donnent tour à tour des marques d'étonnement et d'indignation.*

UN SANS-CULOTTE ROMAIN, *menant* LE PAPE:[38] À genoux, scélérats couronnés! Pour recevoir la bénédiction du saint père: car il n'y a qu'un prêtre capable d'absoudre vos forfaits dont il fut le complice et l'agent perfide. Eh! Dans quelle trame odieuse, dans quelle intrigue criminelle les prêtres et leur chef n'ont-ils pas pris part, n'ont-ils pas joué un rôle? C'est ce monstre à triple couronne, qui, sous main, provoqua une croisade meurtrière contre les Français, comme jadis ses prédécesseurs en avaient conseillé une contre les Sarrazins. Après les rois, les prêtres sont ceux qui firent le plus de mal à la terre et à l'espèce humaine.

Grâces, grâces immortelles soient rendues au peuple français, qui le premier, parmi les modernes, rappela le patriotisme de Brutus[39] et démasqua la tartufferie des augures. Les Français firent rougir les Romains de l'encens qu'ils prostituaient aux pieds d'un prêtre dans le capitole, là même où l'ambitieux César fut poignardé par des mains vertueuses et républicaines.

LE PAPE: Ah! Ah! Vous chargez le tableau . . . Citez un seul de mes prédécesseurs qui ait fait preuve d'autant de modération que moi. À leur exemple, j'aurais bien pu mettre en interdit tout le royaume de France . . .

LE SANS-CULOTTE FRANÇAIS, *l'interrompt*: Dis la république.

---

38. Pape Pie VI (1717–1799): né Giovanni Angelico Braschi, il dirige les États pontificaux de 1775 à sa mort en 1799.
39. Marcus Junius Brutus (vers 85–42 av. J.-C.): politicien romain célèbre pour son rôle dans l'assassinat de Jules César, après que celui-ci s'est déclaré dictateur perpétuel. Pendant la Révolution, son nom est synonyme de résistance héroïque à la tyrannie.

LE PAPE: Eh bien, la république soit! La république. J'aurais pu appeler sur la tête de tous les Français les vengeances du ciel; je me suis contenté de conjurer contre eux toutes les puissances de la terre. Un prêtre pouvait-il moins? Écoutez; faites-moi grâce; tout le reste de ma vie je prierai Dieu pour les sans-culottes.

LE SANS-CULOTTE ROMAIN: Non, non, non! Nous ne voulons plus de prières d'un prêtre: le Dieu des sans-culottes, c'est la liberté, c'est l'égalité, c'est la fraternité! Tu ne connus et ne connaîtras jamais ces dieux-là. Va plutôt exorciser le volcan qui doit dans peu te punir et nous venger.

UN SANS-CULOTTE FRANÇAIS, *après avoir fait ranger en demi-cercle tous les* ROIS, *et avant de les quitter*: Monstres couronnés! Vous auriez dû, sur des échafauds, mourir tous de mille morts: mais où se serait-il trouvé des bourreaux qui eussent consenti à souiller leurs mains dans votre sang vil et corrompu? Nous vous livrons à vos remords, ou plutôt à votre rage impuissante.

Voilà pourtant les auteurs de tous nos maux! Générations à venir, pourrez-vous le croire! Voilà ceux qui tenaient dans leurs mains, qui balançaient les destinées de l'Europe. C'est pour le service de cette poignée de lâches brigands, c'est pour le bon plaisir de ces scélérats couronnés, que le sang d'un million, de deux millions d'hommes, dont le pire valait mieux qu'eux tous, a été versé sur presque tous les points du continent et par-delà les mers. C'est au nom, ou par l'ordre, de cette vingtaine d'animaux féroces que des provinces entières ont été dévastées, des villes populeuses changées en monceaux de cadavres et de cendres, d'innombrables familles violées, mises à nu et réduites à la famine. Ce groupe infâme d'assassins politiques a tenu en échec de grandes nations, et a tourné les uns contre les autres des peuples faits pour être amis et nés pour vivre en frères. Les voilà ces bouchers d'hommes en temps de guerre, ces corrupteurs de l'espèce humaine en temps de paix. C'est du sein des cours de ces êtres immondes que s'exhalait dans les villes et sur les campagnes la contagion de tous les vices; exista-t-il jamais une nation ayant en même temps un roi et des mœurs?

LE PAPE: Il n'y avait pas de mœurs à Rome!... Les cardinaux n'ont point de mœurs!...

LE SANS-CULOTTE FRANÇAIS: Et ces ogres trouvaient des panégyristes et des soutiens! Les prêtres ne donnaient à leur Dieu que les restes de l'encens qu'ils brûlaient aux pieds du prince; et des esclaves chargés de livrées tissues d'or se pavanaient et se croyaient importants quand ils avaient dit: *le roi mon maître* . . . [40] Plus de cent millions d'hommes ont obéi à ces plats tyrans, et tremblaient en prononçant leurs noms avec un saint respect. C'était pour procurer des jouissances à ces mangeurs d'hommes que le peuple, du matin au soir, et d'un bout de l'année à l'autre, travaillait, suait, s'épuisait. Races futures! Pardonnerez-vous à vos bons aïeux cet excès d'avilissement, de stupidité et d'abnégation de soi-même? Nature, hâte-toi d'achever l'œuvre des sans-culottes; souffle ton haleine de feu sur ce rebut de la société, et fais rentrer pour toujours les rois dans le néant d'où ils n'auraient jamais dû sortir.

Fais-y rentrer aussi le premier d'entre nous qui désormais prononcerait le mot *roi* sans l'accompagner des imprécations que l'idée attachée à ce mot infâme présente naturellement à tout esprit républicain.

Pour moi, je m'engage à effacer sur-le-champ du livre des hommes libres quiconque en ma présence souillerait l'air d'une expression qui tendrait à prévenir favorablement

---

40. Voici le sixième et dernier passage, allant de "et des esclaves chargés" jusqu'à "*mon maître*," qui ne fut pas prononcé sur scène.

pour un roi, ou pour toute autre monstruosité de cette
sorte. Camarades, jurons-le tous, et rembarquons-nous.

LES SANS-CULOTTES, *en partant*: Nous le jurons! . . . Vive la
liberté! Vive la république!

SCÈNE VI
Les ROIS d'Europe.

———

FRANÇOIS II: Comme on nous traite, bon Dieu! Avec quelle
indignité! Et qu'allons-nous devenir?

GUILLAUME: Ô mon cher Cagliostro,[41] que n'es-tu ici?
Tu nous tirerais d'embarras.

GEORGE: J'en doute: qu'en pensez-vous, saint-père? Vous
le tenez depuis assez longtemps prisonnier au château
Saint-Ange.[42]

BRASCHI OU LE PAPE: Il ne pourrait rien à tout ceci. Il nous
faudrait quelque chose de surnaturel.

LE ROI D'ESPAGNE: Ah! saint-père, un petit miracle.

LE PAPE: Le temps en est passé . . . Où est-il le bon temps où
les saints traversaient les airs à cheval sur un bâton?

LE ROI D'ESPAGNE: Ô mon parent! Ô Louis XVI! C'est
encore toi qui as eu le meilleur lot. Un mauvais demi-quart
d'heure est bientôt passé! À présent tu n'as plus besoin de
rien. Ici nous manquons de tout: nous sommes entre la

41. Comte Alessandro di Cagliostro (1743–1795): pseudonyme de
l'occultiste italien Joseph Balsamo qui acquit une grande renommée dans
les cours royales d'Europe. Impliqué dans l'affaire du collier de la reine, il
fut incarcéré à la Bastille et expulsé de France avant d'être arrêté par la
Sainte Inquisition en 1789 pour sa pratique de la franc-maçonnerie.
42. Forteresse de Rome qui servit du quatorzième au dix-neuvième siècle
de refuge pour les papes en cas de danger et de tribunal et prison pour les
Etats pontificaux. Cagliostro y fut emprisonné par la Sainte Inquisition.

famine et l'enfer. C'est vous, François et Guillaume, qui nous attirez tout cela. J'ai toujours pensé que cette révolution de France, tôt ou tard, nous jouerait d'un mauvais tour. Il ne fallait pas nous en mêler du tout, du tout.

GUILLAUME: Il vous sied bien, sire d'Espagne, de nous inculper; ne sont-ce pas vos lenteurs ordinaires qui nous ont perdus? Si vous nous aviez secondés à point, c'en était fait de la France.

CATHERINE: Pour moi, je vais me coucher dans cette caverne. Au lieu de vous quereller, qui m'aime me suive . . . Stanislas, ne venez-vous pas me tenir compagnie?

LE ROI DE POLOGNE: Vieille Catau, regarde-toi dans cette fontaine.

CATHERINE: Tu n'as pas toujours été si fier.[43]

L'EMPEREUR: Maudits Français!

LE ROI D'ESPAGNE: Ces sans-culottes que nous méprisions tant d'abord sont pourtant venus à bout de leur dessein. Pourquoi n'en ai-je pas fait un bel autodafé, pour servir d'exemple aux autres?

LE PAPE: Pourquoi ne les ai-je pas excommuniés dès 1789? Nous les avons trop ménagés, trop ménagés.

LE ROI DE NAPLES: Toutes ces réflexions sont belles, mais elles viennent un peu trop tard. Nous sommes dans la galère, il faut ramer: avant tout, il faut manger; occupons-nous, d'abord, de pêche, de chasse ou de labourage.

L'EMPEREUR: Il ferait beau voir l'empereur de la maison d'Autriche gratter la terre pour vivre.

---

43. Stanislas II avait en effet été dans sa jeunesse l'amant de Catherine II et lui devait même son trône.

LE ROI D'ESPAGNE: Aimeriez-vous mieux tirer au sort pour savoir lequel de nous servira de pâture aux autres?

LE PAPE: N'avoir pas même de quoi faire le miracle de la multiplication des pains! Cela ne m'étonne pas, nous avons ici des schismatiques.[44]

CATHERINE: C'est sans doute à moi que ce discours s'adresse: je veux en avoir raison . . . En garde, saint-père.

L'IMPÉRATRICE et LE PAPE se battent, l'une avec son sceptre et l'autre avec sa croix: un coup de sceptre casse la croix; LE PAPE jette sa tiare à la tête de CATHERINE et lui renverse sa couronne. Ils se battent avec leurs chaînes. Le ROI DE POLOGNE veut mettre le holà, en ôtant des mains le sceptre à CATHERINE.

LE ROI DE POLOGNE: Voisine, c'en est assez. Holà! Holà!

L'IMPÉRATRICE: Il te convient bien de m'enlever mon sceptre, lâche! Est-ce pour te dédommager du tien que tu as laissé couper en trois ou quatre morceaux?[45]

LE PAPE: Catherine, je te demande grâce, *escolta mi*:[46] si tu me laisses tranquille, je te donnerai l'absolution pour tous tes péchés.

L'IMPÉRATRICE: L'absolution! Faquin de prêtre! Avant que je te laisse tranquille, il faut que tu avoues et que tu répètes après moi qu'un prêtre, qu'un pape est un charlatan, un joueur de gobelets . . . Allons, répète!

LE PAPE: Un prêtre . . . un pape . . . est un charlatan . . . un joueur de gobelets.

44. Quiconque se sépare d'une confession religieuse et reconnait une autorité spirituelle différente.
45. La phrase "couper en trois ou quatre morceaux" fait référence au deuxième partage de la Pologne en 1793.
46. Erreur probable de Maréchal: la forme correcte devrait être *ascoltami* ("écoute-moi" en italien).

LE ROI D'ESPAGNE, *à part, dans un coin du théâtre*: Quelle trouvaille! J'ai encore un reste de la ration de pain qu'on me donnait à fond de cale. Quel trésor! Il n'y a point de roupies, point de piastres qui vaillent un morceau de pain noir, quand on meurt de faim.

LE ROI DE POLOGNE: Cousin, que fais-tu là à l'écart? Tu manges je crois, j'en retiens part.

L'IMPÉRATRICE et les autres ROIS se jettent sur celui d'Espagne pour lui arracher son morceau de pain.

Et moi aussi, et moi aussi, et moi aussi.

LE ROI DE NAPLES: Que diraient les sans-culottes, s'ils voyaient tous les rois d'Europe se disputer un morceau de pain noir?

Les ROIS se battent: la terre est jonchée de débris de chaînes, de sceptres, de couronnes; les manteaux sont en haillons.

SCÈNE VII
Les acteurs précédents et les SANS-CULOTTES.

———

Les SANS-CULOTTES, qui ont voulu jouir de loin de l'embarras des ROIS réduits à la famine, reviennent dans l'île pour y rouler une barrique de biscuit au milieu des rois affamés.

L'UN DES SANS-CULOTTES, *en défonçant la barrique, et renversant le biscuit*: Tenez, faquins, voilà de la pâture. Bouffez. Le proverbe qui dit: *Il faut que tout le monde vive*, n'a pas été fait pour vous, car il n'y a pas de nécessité que des rois vivent. Mais les sans-culottes sont aussi susceptibles de pitié que de justice. Repaissez-vous donc de ce biscuit de mer, jusqu'à ce que vous soyez acclimatés dans ce pays.

SCÈNE VIII

LES ROIS *se jettent sur le biscuit.*

————

L'IMPÉRATRICE: Un moment! Moi, comme impératrice et propriétaire du domaine le plus vaste, il me faut la plus grande part.

LE ROI DE POLOGNE: Catherine n'a jamais fait petite bouche: mais nous ne sommes plus ici à Pétersbourg; chacun le sien.

LE ROI DE NAPLES: Oui! Oui! Chacun le sien. Cette barrique de biscuit ne doit pas ressembler à la soi-disant république de Pologne.

LE ROI DE PRUSSE *donne un coup de sceptre sur les doigts de* L'IMPÉRATRICE.

L'IMPÉRATRICE: Tais-toi, ravisseur de la Silésie.[47]

LE PAPE: Messieurs! Messieurs! Rendez à César ce qui est à César.

L'IMPÉRATRICE: Si tu rendais à César ce qui appartient à César, petit évêque de Rome! . . .

L'EMPEREUR: La paix, la paix: il y en a pour tout le monde.

LE ROI DE PRUSSE: Oui, mais il n'y en aura pas pour longtemps.

LE ROI DE NAPLES: Mais voilà le volcan qui paraît vouloir nous mettre tous d'accord: une lave brûlante descend du cratère et s'avance vers nous. Dieux!

————

47. La Silésie est une région en Europe centrale, située principalement aujourd'hui dans le Sud-Ouest de la Pologne. De 1740 à 1763, elle fit l'objet de nombreuses batailles entre l'Autriche de Marie-Thérèse et la Prusse de Frédéric II. C'est la Prusse qui l'emportera et "ravira" ainsi la Silésie.

LE ROI D'ESPAGNE: Bonne Notre-Dame! Secourez-moi . . .
Si j'en réchappe, je me fais sans-culotte.

LE PAPE: Et moi je prends femme.

CATHERINE: Et moi je passe aux Jacobins ou aux Cordeliers.[48]

Le volcan commence son éruption: il jette sur le théâtre des pierres, des charbons brûlants . . . etc.

L'explosion se fait: le feu assiège les ROIS *de toutes parts; ils tombent, consumés dans les entrailles de la terre entr'ouverte.*

FIN

48. Catherine II fait ici référence à deux sociétés politiques particulièrement influentes et militantes, affiliées en 1793 à la Montagne: le club des Jacobins et le club des Cordeliers (tous deux ayant reçu leurs noms des anciens couvents où se tenaient leurs réunions).

BIBLIOGRAPHY

PRIMARY SOURCES

Aulard, François, ed. *Recueil des Actes du Comité de Salut Public*. Vol. 8. Paris: Imprimerie nationale, 1895.

Carbon de Flins Des Oliviers, Claude-Marie-Louis-Emmanuel. *Le Réveil d'Épiménide à Paris*. Toulouse: Broulhiet, 1790.

Collé, Charles. *La Partie de chasse de Henri IV*. Paris: Didot, 1778.

Maréchal, Sylvain. *Almanach des Honnêtes Gens*. Paris, 1788.

———. *Anti-Saints: The New Golden Legend of Sylvain Maréchal*. Translated and introduced by Sheila Delany. Edmonton: University of Alberta Press, 2012.

———. *Apologues modernes, à l'usage du dauphin, Premières leçons du fils ainé d'un roi*. Brussels, 1788.

———. *Correctif à la Révolution*. Paris: Chez les Directeurs de l'Imprimerie du Cercle Social, 1793.

———. *Dame Nature à la barre de l'Assemblée Nationale*. Paris: Chez les marchands de nouveauté, 1791.

———. *Hymnes pour les 36 fêtes décadaires*. Paris: Basset, 1794.

———. *La Fête de la Raison*. Paris: C.-F. Patris, 1794.

———. *L'Âge d'Or*. Paris: Chez Guillot, 1782.

———. *Les Antiquités d'Herculanum avec leurs explications en françois*. Paris: Chez David, 1780.

———. *Manifeste des Égaux*. Paris, 1796.

———. *The Woman Priest: A Translation of Sylvain Maréchal's Novella, La Femme Abbé*. Translated and introduced by

Sheila Delany. Edmonton: University of Alberta Press, 2016.

Mercier, Louis-Sébastien. *L'An 2440, rêve s'il en fut jamais.* Londres, 1771.

———. *Le Nouveau Paris.* Vol. 3. Brunswick: Chez les principaux libraires, 1800.

Montesquieu. *Lettres persanes.* Edited by Laurent Versini. Paris: GF Flammarion, 1995.

Paine, Thomas. *Opinion de Thomas Payne sur l'affaire de Louis Capet.* Paris: Imprimerie nationale, 1793.

Palissot, Charles. *The Philosophes.* Edited by Jessica Goodman and Olivier Ferret. Translated by Jessica Goodman, Caitlin Gray, Felicity Gush, Phoebe Jackson, Nina Ludekens, Rosie Rigby, and Lorenzo Edwards-Jones. Cambridge, UK: Open Book Publishers, 2021.

Rousseau, Jean-Jacques. *Du Contrat social.* Edited by Bruno Bernardi. Paris: GF Flammarion, 2001.

BIOGRAPHIES OF SYLVAIN MARÉCHAL

Aubert, Françoise. *Sylvain Maréchal: Passion et Faillite d'un Égalitaire.* Pise-Paris: Goliardica-Nizet, 1975.

Dommanget, Maurice. *Sylvain Maréchal: L'égalitaire, "L'homme sans Dieu," sa vie, son oeuvre (1750–1803).* Paris: Cahiers de Spartacus, 1950.

Fusil, Casimir-Alexandre. *Sylvain Maréchal ou L'Homme sans Dieu, H.S.D, 1750–1803.* Paris: Plon, 1936.

Perovic, Sanja. "Sylvain Maréchal (1750–1803)." The Super-Enlightenment: A Digital Archive. Accessed April 22, 2023. https://exhibits.stanford.edu/super-e/feature/sylvain-marechal-1750-1803.

SECONDARY SOURCES

Ailloud-Nicolas, Catherine. "Scènes de théâtre: *Le Tremblement de terre de Lisbonne* (1755), *Le Jugement dernier des rois* (1793)." In *L'invention de la catastrophe au XVIIIe siècle: Du châtiment divin au désastre naturel,* edited by Anne-Marie Mercier-Faivre and Christiane Thomas, 403–418. Genève: Droz, 2008.

Apostolidès, Jean-Marie. "La guillotine littéraire." *French Review* 63, no. 4 (1989): 598–606.

———. "Theater and Terror: *Le Jugement dernier des rois.*" In *Terror and Consensus: Vicissitudes of French Thought,* edited by Jean-Joseph Goux and Philip R. Wood, 135–144. Stanford, CA: Stanford University Press, 1998.

Avramescu, Cătălin. *An Intellectual History of Cannibalism.* Princeton, NJ: Princeton University Press, 2009.

Baecque, Antoine de. *La Gloire et l'effroi.* Paris: Grasset, 1977.

———. *Les Éclats du rire: La culture des rieurs au XVIIIe siècle.* Paris: Calmann-Lévy, 2000.

Bérard, Suzanne J. "Aspects du théâtre à Paris sous la Terreur." *Revue d'Histoire littéraire de la France,* no. 4/5 (1990): 610–621.

Bianchi, Serge. "Le Théâtre de l'an II (culture et société sous la Révolution)." *Annales historiques de la Révolution française* 278 (1989): 417–432.

Bourdin, Philippe. *Aux Origines du théâtre patriotique.* Paris: CNRS, 2017.

Bruit, Guy. "89–93: Quel Théâtre?" *Raison Présente* 91 (1989): 97–107.

Challamel, Augustin, and Wilhelm Tenint. *Les Français sous la Révolution.* Paris: Challamel Editeur, 1843.

Cot, Guillaume. "La Scène et la Loi: les dramaturgies du droit (1789–1794)." PhD diss., Université Paris VIII, 2021.

Coudreuse, Anne. "Insultes et théâtre de la Terreur: l'exemple du *Jugement dernier des rois* (1793) de Pierre-Sylvain Maréchal." In *Les insultes: bilan et perspectives, théorie et actions,* edited by Dominique Lagorgette, 30–36. Chambéry, France: Presses universitaires Savoie Mont Blanc, 2016.

Darlow, Mark. "Staging the Revolution: The Fait historique." In "Revolutionary Culture: Continuity and Change," edited by

Mark Darlow, special issue, *Nottingham French Studies* 45, no. 1 (Spring 2006): 77–88.

Dibie, Pascal. "Le peuple fait le spectacle: Le théâtre révolutionnaire de Pierre Sylvain Maréchal (1750–1803)." In *Le peuple existe-t-il?*, edited by Michel Wieviorka, 83–99. Auxerre, France: Éditions Sciences Humaines, 2012.

Didier, Béatrice. "*Le Jugement dernier des Rois* de Sylvain Maréchal." In *Écrire la Révolution (1789–1799)*, edited by Béatrice Didier, 171–180. Paris: Presses Universitaires de France, 1989.

———. "Sylvain Maréchal et le *Jugement dernier des rois*." In *Saint-Denis ou le Jugement dernier des rois*, edited by Roger Bourderon, 129–138. Saint-Denis, France: Editions PSD Saint-Denis, 1993.

Edelstein, Dan. "The Egyptian French Revolution: Freemasonry, Antiquarianism, and the Mythology of Nature." In *The Super-Enlightenment: Daring to Know Too Much*, edited by Dan Edelstein, 215–241. Oxford: Voltaire Foundation, 2010.

Estrée, Paul d'. *Le Théâtre sous la Terreur*. Paris: Émile-Paul frères, 1913.

Fournier, Stéphanie. *Rire au théâtre à Paris à la fin du XVIIIe siècle*. Collection L'Europe des Lumières. Paris: Classiques Garnier, 2016.

Frantz, Pierre. "Rire et théâtre carnavalesque pendant la Révolution." *Dix-Huitième Siècle* 32 (2000): 291–306.

Gaudemer, Marjorie. "La dramaturgie propagandiste, étude de cinq pièces militantes de la Terreur." Master's thesis, Université Paris X, 2001–2002.

Goldzink, Jean. *Comique et comédie au siècle des Lumières*. Paris: L'Harmattan, 2000.

Graczyk, Annette. "Le théâtre de la Révolution française, média de masses entre 1789 et 1794." *Dix-huitième Siècle* 21 (1989): 395–409.

Guedj, Aimé. "L'internationalisme républicain de Sylvain Maréchal ou *Le Jugement dernier des rois*." In *Le Cheminement de l'idée européenne dans les idéologies de la paix et de la guerre*, edited by Marita Gilli, 75–90. Besançon, France: Presses de l'Université de Franche-Comté, 1991.

Hallays-Dabot, Victor. *Histoire de la censure théâtrale en France*. Paris: E. Dentu, 1862.

Hamiche, Daniel. *Le Théâtre et la Révolution: La lutte de classes au théâtre en 1789 et 1793*. Paris: Union Générale d'Editions, 1973.

Huet, Marie-Hélène. *The Culture of Disaster*. Chicago: University of Chicago Press, 2012.

Hunt, Lynn. *The Family Romance of the French Revolution*. Berkeley: University of California Press, 1992.

Hyslop, Beatrice F. "The Theater during a Crisis: The Parisian Theater during the Reign of Terror." *The Journal of Modern History* 17, no. 4 (1945): 332–355.

Jauffret, Paul Eugène. *Le Théatre Révolutionnaire (1788–1799)*. Paris: Furne, Jouvet, 1869.

Jomand-Baudry, Régine. "Désacralisation et transfert du sacré dans *Le Jugement dernier des rois* de Sylvain Maréchal." In *Le Sacré en question. Bible et mythes sur les scènes du xviiie siècle*, edited by Béatrice Ferrier, 235–251. Paris: Classiques Garnier, 2015.

Kennedy, Emmet, Marie-Laurence Netter, James P. McGregor, and Mark V. Olsen. *Theatre, Opera, and Audiences in Revolutionary Paris: Analysis and Repertory*. Westport, CT: Greenwood Press, 1996.

Lumière, Henry. *Le Théâtre français pendant la Révolution*. Paris: Dentu, 1894.

Mannucci, Erica Joy. "The Anti-patriot Patriarch: Utopianism in Sylvain Maréchal." *History of European Ideas* 16, no. 4–6 (1993): 627–632.

———. "Revolution and the Last Judgement." In *The Languages of Revolution*, edited by L. Valtz Mannucci, 227–244. Milan: Università degli studi di Milano, 1989.

Matyaszewski, Paweł. "La possibilité d'une île, ou le *Jugement dernier des rois* de Sylvain Maréchal (1793)." *Cahiers ERTA* 22 (2020): 71–88.

McCallam, David. *Volcanoes in Eighteenth-Century Europe: An Essay in Environmental Humanities.* Oxford University Studies in the Enlightenment. Liverpool: Liverpool University Press, 2019.

McCready, Susan. "Performing Time in the Revolutionary Theater." *Dalhousie French Studies* 55 (2001): 26–30.

Miller, Mary Ashburn. *A Natural History of Revolution: Violence and Nature in the French Revolutionary Imagination, 1789–1794.* Ithaca, NY: Cornell University Press, 2011.

Moland, Louis. *Théâtre de la Révolution.* Paris: Garnier frères, 1877.

Nadeau, Martin. "La politique culturelle de l'an II: les infortunes de la propagande révolutionnaire au théâtre." *Annales historiques de la Révolution française* 327 (January–March 2002): 57–74.

Ozouf, Mona. *Festivals and the French Revolution.* Translated by Alan Sheridan. Cambridge, MA: Harvard University Press, 1988.

Perovic, Sanja. *The Calendar in Revolutionary France: Perceptions of Time in Literature, Culture, Politics.* Cambridge: Cambridge University Press, 2012.

Proust, Jacques. "De Sylvain Maréchal à Maiakovski: Contribution à l'étude du théâtre révolutionnaire." In *Studies in Eighteenth-Century French Literature*, 215–224. Exeter, UK: University of Exeter Press, 1975.

———. "Le Jugement dernier des rois." In *Approches des Lumières*, 371–379. Paris: Klincksieck, 1974.

Robert, Yann. *Dramatic Justice: Trial by Theater in the Age of the French Revolution.* Philadelphia: University of Pennsylvania Press, 2019.

Rodmell, Graham E. *French Drama of the Revolutionary Years.* London: Routledge, 1990.

Sagan, Eli. *Citizens and Cannibals: The French Revolution, the Struggle for Modernity, and the Origins of Ideological Terror.* New York: Rowman & Littlefield Publishers, 2001.

Sajous D'Oria, Michèle. "Les bouffons des rois." In *La Participation dramatique: Spectacle et espace théâtral (1730–1830),* 237–267. Collection L'Europe des Lumières. Paris: Classiques Garnier, 2020.

Tissier, André. *Les Spectacles à Paris pendant la Révolution.* Geneva: Droz, 2002.

Truchet, Jacques. *Théâtre du XVIIIe siècle.* Vol. 2. Collection Bibliothèque de la Pléiade. Paris: Gallimard, 1974.

Zatorska, Izabella. "De l'utopie à la prophétie: la mutation de l'utopie dans le théâtre de la Révolution." *Romanica Wratislaviensia* 35 (1992): 15–23.

ABOUT THE EDITOR

YANN ROBERT is an associate professor in the Department of French and Francophone Studies at the University of Illinois, Chicago. He is the author of *Dramatic Justice: Trial by Theater in the Age of the French Revolution* and a critical edition of the revolutionary play *L'Ami des lois*. His research has received support from the Andrew W. Mellon Foundation, notably through a two-year postdoctoral fellowship at Stanford University and a one-year research fellowship at the Newberry Library, as well as from the Jacob K. Javits and the Mrs. Giles Whiting Foundations. His current research focuses on vigilantism and popular justice in the literature and culture of Enlightenment and Revolutionary France.